True Savage 3

Chris Green

**Lock Down Publications and Ca$h
Presents**
True Savage 3
A Novel by *Chris Green*

Chris Green

Lock Down Publications
P.O. Box 870494
Mesquite, Tx 75187

Copyright 2018 True Savage 3

Lock Down Publications
Like our page on Facebook: Lock Down Publications
@
www.facebook.com/lockdownpublications.ldp
Cover design and layout by: **Dynasty Cover Me**
Book interior design by: **Shawn Walker**
Edited by: **Sunny Giovanni**

Stay Connected with Us!

Text **LOCKDOWN** to 22828 to stay up-to-date with new releases, sneak peaks, contests and more...

Thank you!

Chris Green

Submission Guideline.

Submit the first three chapters of your completed manuscript to ldpsubmissions@gmail.com, subject line: Your book's title. The manuscript must be in a .doc file and sent as an attachment. Document should be in Times New Roman, double spaced and in size 12 font. Also, provide your synopsis and full contact information. If sending multiple submissions, they must each be in a separate email.

Have a story but no way to send it electronically? You can still submit to LDP/Ca$h Presents. Send in the first three chapters, written or typed, of your completed manuscript to:

LDP: Submissions Dept
Po Box 870494
Mesquite, Tx 75187

DO NOT send original manuscript. Must be a duplicate.

Provide your synopsis and a cover letter containing your full contact information.

Thanks for considering LDP and Ca$h Presents.

Acknowledgments

I would like to thank every friend and family member who stood by me through this process. My big brother Micheal Brown aka Bang. Jabari Burton aka JB. Adonis Matthews aka Westside .Osama, Five, World and the rest of the family Dons.

I would like to thank the beautiful Princess Eatmon for all your support and motivation since I've been incarcerated. I love you. My auntie Candies Green. My great granny, Doris Mathis, and, of course, my mother and daughter.

Thank you to the entire LOCK DOWN PUBLICATIONS squad. Ca$h, without you, I don't know if I would be able to keep striving inside this industry. Your words and encouragement are molding me day by day. I thank you for the oppurtunity and in my opinion, the fatherly wisdom. With that, I will forever respect you and remember these days of my first steps to success.

Finally, to all my readers: I love you very much and will continue to forever. I hope you all enjoy this latest street story of mine.

Chris Green

Chapter 1

"How in the fuck did this happen?" Ghost asked, looking at Tiffany and Suave as he held the phone.

"Baby, I swear she's only been gone for a few hours. I didn't think nothing would happen to her just from heading to the store," she said on the verge of tears.

"Hold up, let's just think for a second. It's no way in fuck someone could just snatch her up out of the blue. Think about it. We only been back to Atlanta for one day," D-Lo said.

"That means someone had to been watching us. We all left on different days. It's kind of impossible for someone to follow us all the way from California, back to Atlanta, and know exactly where our duck off spot is without us scoping them out," Suave replied.

D-Lo slightly cut his eyes at Tiffany as she sat twiddling her fingers. "Whoa, bruh, let me mobb at you for a second," he spoke as they moved away from the crowd.

While everyone sat around trying to understand the twisted predicament, D-Lo and Ghost made their way into the small kitchen.

"I don't think Tiffany's being honest with you, bro," he accused with a strong feeling on his brain.

"What do you mean?" Ghost responded, thinking hard about Erica. He knew in his heart that something was already harmfully done. He didn't even know the people he was dealing with, which made it even more complicated.

"The day we dropped them off at the airport, she never left. Me and Shadow spotted her the next day, after we dropped Suave and the kids off."

"What do you mean? Didn't y'all drop them both off and watch them get on the plane?" Ghost asked confusingly.

"What we thought we seen wasn't real because she damn sure made her way on the plane with Suave, trying to stay unnoticed."

Ghost moved past his brother and made his way back into the living room where the rest of the family stood in silence.

"Yo, Pop, you and Suave step outside and holla at me real quick," D-Lo mumbled, opening the front door.

As the three of them headed towards the porch, Suave grabbed Mariah, sensing the hard aura in the air.

Ghost walked over to Tiffany and stood in front of her as the door closed, leaving them alone. "You better start explaining what the fuck is going on, right now," he said, bending down in front of Tiffany.

"Daddy, what the fuck are you talking about? I'm just as lost as you," she replied with an annoyed look on her face.

Ghost brought his left hand down hard, slapping her to the floor. She reacted instantly, jumping back to her feet and delivered two punches directly to his jaw, before she realized what was going on. Her legs were in the air as her back came crashing down to the floor, knocking the wind completely out of her.

"Chancee! What the fuck is wrong with you?" she uttered, trying to catch her breath as the tears poured from her eyes.

"I said tell me what the fuck is going on," he demanded, not feeling any sympathy as he held his hand around her throat.

"You think I really had something to do with her getting fucking kidnapped, Ghost?" Tiffany whined with her lips trembling in fear.

"No, I don't. But I want to know why the fuck you weren't on the plane with Erica when she left California."

Tiffany held Ghost's arm as she stared into his eyes and knew the lies couldn't be contained anymore. So many things occurred within the time she was dealing with him that the pieces began to fall slowly, and disintegrate everything they worked so hard to build.

"I stayed to save you Chance. I did what I had to do to make sure you came home to us," Tiffany said with a small line of blood running down her cheek.

"What in the fuck are you talking about, Tiff?" he asked, feeling the annoyance scrub against his temper.

Tiffany's green eyes locked as she stared at Ghost and let it all go. "I'm the one who killed Romeo."

Ghost's eyes stiffened when hearing his cousin's name as the flashback at the warehouse replayed through his brain slowly.

He remembered the bullet that pierced Romeo's body, killing him instantly. The picture of the man's lifeless face ran through his eyes as he thought about Shadow saying that he didn't pull the trigger.

"I knew you wouldn't be able to kill him, Chance. If I wouldn't have stayed and got on that plane that night, I probably would be preparing your funeral right now," Tiffany said with the truth coming deeply from her heart.

"You're fucking lying. That is something that I just can't go for. You expect me to believe that you killed Romeo, Tiffany? Huh? All this hard work I put in to end this shit and you want to sit here and play mental with me?" Ghost asked as he pulled his pistol from his waist.

Tiffany gasped with her eyes glued to the gun. She took a deep breath and told Ghost what he wanted to know.

"When I was sixteen, my parents were murdered in their car, sitting in the driveway. They were shot numerous times and their bodies were sat on fire as I sat and watched from the window of my bedroom. My older brother Jimmie was currently serving a bid in a county jail and wasn't aware of the situation until he came home. I was only sixteen, I had nowhere to go and no one to take me in. The last of my family was Jimmie's stepmom and she hated my guts, so I was forced into an orphanage. I stayed in that institution for six months until the director told me to pack my things one day."

"Keep going," Ghost said, still holding her just in case she thought about lying to his face anymore.

"The day I left the orphanage, I was given a plane ticket to California with three hundred dollars and an address attached to it. At first, I refused to leave, but the director of the home told me that I didn't have a choice. He told me he found me a home and I was getting adopted. He promised me that everything would be okay, hugged me and dropped me off at the airport. When I arrived in LA, a limo was waiting for me as I stepped my first foot outside of the sliding doors. The man greeted me with a head nod as he opened the car door for me and guarded me inside. I had never been to California, so I was clueless on where I was headed until I pulled up in front of my new home. When I got out of the limo, I was escorted to the door where I met my new father."

"Pablo?" Ghost asked, clenching his jaws.

The small tear that left Tiffany's right eye told him that he was right as she shook her head yes.

"Keep fucking going," Ghost yelled, itching to shoot her directly between her eyes.

Tiffany wiped the blood from her cheek and continued to speak. "Pablo adopted me and took me in. Within the first few weeks of being with him, he started to fill me in on his way of life. He told me the only thing I was made for was to go to school."

"Be more specific," Ghost replied angrily, pulling the hammer of the gun back slowly.

Tiffany watched Ghost's trigger finger from the side of her eye as she relaxed and finished what she was saying. "I went to school at the Orient, aka Asia," she said, barely above a whisper.

"What in the fuck is that? Stop beating around the fucking bush with me before I lose my patience with you, bitch," he said, feeling destroyed by her deceit.

"It's a training school for assassins. Romeo went to school with me. We were both sectioned in Class E3. I graduated head of my class and Romeo graduated second. I'm sorry Chance, I didn't know he was related to you." Tiffany spilled out with a look of sincerity in her eyes.

"Who the fuck are you?" Ghost asked with a look of hurt and disappointment written on his face.

"I'm your woman. I'm the same fucking person, Ghost. I just didn't want to put any more pressure on you," Tiffany yelled truthfully, trying to get him to understand.

Ghost looked down at her sadly as he slowly removed his gun from her face. After he released his hand from around her neck, she got off the floor and looked him eye to eye as she pushed the small layer of hair out of her vision.

"You're no different from Erica. You've been around me this entire time and constantly lied instead of being real with me. Your loyalty never existed. Were you paid to come kill me? Huh?"

Tiffany's eyes began to well back up as she looked in his eyes. "No, no." She kept repeating, shaking her head.

"I don't wanna be with you anymore. Take care of my kids until this is all done. You and Erica already have a private account in the Virgin Islands, and the house is already paid for. It's no reason for you to contact me anymore."

"Ghost, don't say that to me," she cried wiping her tears away.

"I don't trust you anymore. I think it's better if we just stay away from each other," Ghost said, opening the door to walk out.

"Chance, don't leave me like this," Tiffany cried as the door slammed in her face.

Suave, D-Lo and their father, Michael, stood outside in the driveway when Ghost appeared out of the house. The look he wore on his face made D-Lo's stomach ache as he felt the worst had just occurred in the house between Ghost and Tiffany.

"Suave, take Mariah back in the house to her. We need to get away from here like now. I'm starting to get to the point where I don't trust anyone," Ghost said, pulling the hood to his black leather vest on.

"Listen, bro, this shit is starting to get a little out of our league. We're not gonna be able to survive another war in a totally different state. We have too much on our plate," D-Lo said.

"My fuckin' bitch probably laying somewhere dead right now and you talking about too much on our plate? I've built this shit by hand, made me a family, and my shit is falling down in front of my eyes," Ghost screamed loudly.

The gray clouds in the sky began to form together as a strip of lightning lit up the area.

"I never meant it like that, bro," D-Lo said, feeling that Ghost was about to turn up.

Michael stood silently as his two sons went back and forth with each other. He wanted to ease the problem that he saw escalating, but every time he tried to speak, they grew louder.

"So, what did you mean it like, huh? Fuck nigga, this is my shit. The only one catching all the fucking problems is me," Ghost said, walking up into D-Lo's face.

"I think you need to chill the fuck out boy, before you end up making me mad with that mouth, lil' bro. I'm starting not to even wanna be around you anymore. Regardless of how much you win, you always want more. You're the reason your bitch is probably dead right now," D-Lo said through clenched teeth.

"Listen, you two need to chill the fuck out. This isn't the time to be going against each other," Michael said.

"I'm the reason my bitch is gonna get back home, scary ass nigga. The same scary ass nigga that let a rat into our circle to kill our own mother." Ghost ranted, looking into his brother's eyes.

The words that left Ghost's mouth was the fuel to D-Lo's fire, making him swing the first punch, striking Ghost on the cheek. He followed up with one more as Ghost scooped him off his feet, caving his back into the ground.

"Dis what you want, motherfucker?" Ghost asked, wildly crashing his fist down onto D-Lo's temple twice.

D-Lo blocked the third hit with his elbow as he grabbed his brother's arm and pulled him to the ground.

The rain began to pour violently as Tiffany and Suave ran out of the house to the scene.

"Bae, D-Lo, stop," Tiffany cried as she tried to break them apart.

Michael pulled her back, shaking his head, as he watched his two sons fight as if they weren't even related.

D-Lo head butted Ghost, pushing him on his side, making his gun slide from his waist line and hit the ground. Climbing on top of him, he struck him three times in the face before Michael snatched him off his little brother.

The raindrops that danced on his face were the only things that kept him conscious as he rolled over and grabbed his gun off the concrete.

"Ghost, no," Tiffany screamed as he placed the gun between his brother's eyes, standing to his feet.

D-Lo stared down the barrel of the gun as his brother's finger wrapped around the trigger. "So, you gonna shoot me, nigga? I've been the main one by your fucking side this whole time," D-Lo cursed with spit flying out the side of his mouth.

Michael sat quietly as he watched Ghost's finger closely in case he had to make a jump for his gun.

"Fuck you, nigga, I'm the real don of all this shit. I started this shit and I'm the reason these niggas respect us!" Ghost yelled through his slightly swollen jaw.

"Well go-ahead, Don, kill the last brother you got. The rest of our family is dead. Let's end the rest of it right here," D-Lo replied with his heartrate rising.

The eyes of Ghost were as black as death as his heart felt like it was turning to stone. He gripped the pistol harder as he started to tighten his jaw bone. Michael, Suave and Tiffany continued to look in shock as Ghost stood in the rain with the look of death aimed at his brother.

"Son. Just put the gun down," Michael said, seeing the same look that reminded him of his younger days. He knew at that moment Ghost was in a state of mind where he could easily do something he really didn't want to.

"Please, bro, just listen and chill, he's your brother, not your enemy," Suave said, seeing Ghost bite his bottom lip.

Twan's bloody face flashed through Ghost's membrane as his right eye twitched. His hand began to slowly shake as the memory of his mother's dead body flipped past his eyes. His heart began to thump harder as he pictured his older brother laying in front of him with his eyes fully open. The darkness that was taking over his head began to fade slowly as a tear fell down his left eye.

D-Lo noticed his little brother's hand starting to tremble but remained in fear of being shot. He knew that his brother loved him, but he also knew that his temper could bring the world crashing down.

"We all we got, Ghost," D-Lo said, looking at his brother with hurt in his heart.

Ghost stared hard in his brother's eyes before he slowly let the pistol fall to his side. "I'm all I got," he said, pulling his hoodie over his head and walking to the car.

After he got in, he crank up the Challenger and left out of the parking lot with his car tires screeching.

D-Lo closed his eyes for a second and took a deep breath from the situation that just took place. He knew that Ghost was hurt and he knew that the way he was moving, there were only more problems that were waiting ahead.

"We have to find him and calm this down so we can get Erica back," Tiffany said with sadness written on her face.

"I don't know what to do anymore. He's not gonna listen to me or anybody else when it comes down to it. He's probably never going to talk to me again," D-Lo said, looking at Tiffany.

"We have to stop him before he gets himself killed," she said, looking at all three men like they were oblivious to what was going on.

"He's not gonna listen. Chance's mind is set a certain way and he's willing to die before he gives anyone else the satisfaction of thinking he is wrong. He's lost contact with the environment and his personality is disintegrated. He's not gonna stop until he gets Erica back," Michael voiced.

"I'm not understanding what you're saying," Tiffany said, wondering what any of that had to do with Ghost being on a rampage.

Michael sighed and looked Tiffany in her eyes as they all stood around and listened. "Chance is schizophrenic. When he was younger, I thought that he was just terrible because he was my son, but it was worse than I thought. Before he turned four, he used to have little blackout spells, but it wasn't the average shit you would see for a child who hadn't turned four yet. I have the same blackouts to this day, but I've learned to control it more than it controlling me," Michael said with a stern expression.

"Why would you let everyone know that shit, pop? It's none of their business about bro's issue," D-Lo said, feeling it was too much going on already with Ghost.

"First off, everyone is not here. Secondly, I assume that all of you are close if you're a part of this thing you have going on with each other. Ghost is sick, but he's a brilliant individual. He's my son. We're not going to fix anything if everyone is walking around clueless of what the issue is. Now that we know, we have to excuse Chance for his actions and stand behind him or watch him commit suicide," Michael said sternly.

The pain Tiffany held inside from what Chance's father just said was unbearable. Ghost really felt alone and he felt that no one was by his side from the start. She always wondered why one minute his mind was so persuasive and genuine, then the next he would want to kill everything moving.

"We have to help him, D-Lo," Tiffany said, looking back and forth between the three men.

"All we have to do is get the fifty million dollars I have and pay the ransom for the girl. It's no other option when we were dealing with these people," Michael replied in a calm voice.

"And who exactly are we dealing with?" D-Lo asked, feeling the pressure about to kick back in soon.

"Pauly the Butcher. He's a leader of a Sicilian mafia family. He's the real deal when it comes down to business and his money. He was one of Jesus's buyers and I robbed him for the same fifty million dollars that he's telling Chance he wants in return of this woman. The problem isn't the money, it's the hundred keys that we don't have," Michael said, looking at them.

D-Lo looked at Tiffany as if the thought popped in their head at the same time. She instantly pulled out her phone, dialing Ghost's number. She got the voicemail back to back and scrolled down the call log until she reached Pablo's name. Dialing his number, she placed the phone to her ear and waited for an answer.

The funny accent from the woman that answered the phone caught her off guard as she looked at the front screen to make sure she had the right number.

"Can I speak to Pablo?" Tiffany asked with an aggravated look.

D-Lo observed her expression change as she listened to the person on the other end of her cell.

"Are you serious?" Tiffany asked in a hurt tone as she lowered her head.

Hanging the phone up, Tiffany slid it in her back pocket as she wiped the tears that dropped from her eyes.

"What happened?" D-Lo questioned, seeing her mood flip.

"Pablo's dead," Tiffany mumbled as she continued to cry.

"Fuck," D-Lo yelled loudly, knowing Pablo was their last hope to run across two hundred keys. The thought of Erica being killed popped through his mind as he thought hard on a new plan.

Chapter 2

Ghost stepped out of his Challenger and jogged through the rain to the front door of the house. After shaking the irritating rain droplets off his clothes, he rang the doorbell and stepped back. He looked at the camera out the corner of his eye as the locks to the door opened.

The maid never felt her life exit her body when Ghost shot her in the eye with the silenced .45 automatic handgun. Stepping in the house, Ghost pushed her body with his foot as he closed the door, looking around the massive crib. He stepped over the woman's body and headed towards the double doors to the living room.

Red sat on the couch, watching the sixty-inch HD plasma that hung on his mantel piece. A green Garcia Vega burned in between his finger and a small glass of Grey Goose rested in his other hand. As he took a sip of his drink, the power in the house shut off, leaving him in complete darkness.

"Godammit, Marriana?" Red yelled out as he flicked the power button to the remote over and over. He raised off the couch and headed towards the door that led to his hallway.

Sliding them open, the body of his maid fell headfirst to the hardwood floor.

"What the fuck?" Red shouted, jumping back and falling over the small step that led to the center of the room.

When he saw Ghost step through the double doors, his heart exploded with fear as he stared down the eyes of a soul that he used to know.

"Ghost, what the fuck are you doing in my house?" Red yelled, trying to ease his way backwards.

Boc! Ghost's gun clapped, ringing through Red's shoulder.

"Oh, God! Aghh fuck!" Red panicked as he covered the small hole that began to pour blood from his flesh.

"You know what the fuck I want, Red," Ghost replied with the barrel of the gun aimed at his head.

"Is this about money, bro? You can fucking have it, Ghost. You can have it," he said, trembling in fear from the pain of the bullet.

The barrel of Ghost's gun crashed across Red's head, making stars appear in his vision. He held his hands out in front of him as he tried to shake the dizziness from his eyes.

"I want them bricks, bitch, I got money, stupid ass nigga," Ghost said, snatching him back and forth by the collar of his shirt.

"It's under the kitchen counter, Ghost. Just chill, bro, please," Red whimpered with his eye swelling profusely.

"You know the routine, bitch. Get up and get it. You try anything dumb, the brightness to yo' life gonna click out like a dead lightbulb," Ghost said, picking him up by the back of his shirt.

"Ghost, I never betrayed you, my nigga. I stood by you when no one else would."

As they stepped into the kitchen, Red tripped over the second maid that laid on the floor with a knife inside the back of her head. Ghost flashed him an evil smile as he pointed his gun towards the cabinet. Red felt his heart beat through his shirt as he eased down to the bottom of the sink.

"Keep them fingers tight now," Ghost ranted, playing with Red's head as he gripped the pistol harder.

"I ain't playing no games with you, Ghost," Red replied, pulling the duffel bag of cocaine from the spot.

"Unzip it, nigga," Ghost yelled, startling him as he was sitting on his knees.

Red sighed in relief as he opened the bag, revealing the packaged drugs. The bricks laid neatly on top of each other in three different rows.

"How many is it?" Ghost asked, looking down inside the bag.

"It's twenty-one keys, bro. Just take it and leave," Red said, feeling his arm turn numb.

"That's twenty-one keys right there?" Ghost asked, being funny as he eased the hammer to the gun back.

Red kept his hands visible as he nodded in silence.

Ghost pushed him to the floor as he grabbed the bag and zipped it up. "How you wanna die?" He asked, putting the bag on his back.

Red's eyes instantly began to tear up as he started begging. "I gave you what I had, Ghost. You don't have to do this."

Toot, toot, toot, toot, toot! The silenced gun sparked, with bullets crashing against Red's skull. As he laid stiffly on the floor, Ghost watched eagerly to see if he would flinch. Satisfied with the quietness he received, he began to wipe down anything he accidently touched as he made his way back through the front door. Ghost was on a mission for those keys, and if that was what Erica was worth, then the city got their grim reaper back.

Brooklyn, New York

The wind was cutting thick early in the afternoon on 21st and Church Street. Dev was posted on the corner by the stop sign as he looked back and forth down the two-way street. He pulled his fitted cap down tighter when he spotted the man he was after coming out of the house. Dev removed his Glock 9 from his waistband and crossed the street to where the man walked freely. The victim never knew what hit him until he walked into Dev's barrel.

Bloc! Bloc! Bloc! Bloc! Bloc! Bloc! Bloc! The 9-millimeter clapped, killing the man instantly. Dev stepped over his slumped body, putting another slug into the man's throat as his phone sounded off. Pulling his phone out his jacket pocket, he looked at his surroundings and down at the message.

"Come to the spot now," Dev read silently, looking at Lockz's name on the screen.

Dev tossed the phone back in his jacket and headed back to the alleyway across the street.

Pooch sat outside the corner with four Harlem niggas, shooting dice on the sidewall by New York Avenue. He watched intensively as the man shook the dice smoothly in his hand, letting them glide off his fingers. When the dice stopped, the dealers cheered with happiness, picking up their money from their side bets.

"You gotta be a little fresher, son," the man said, picking up his winnings.

"It's all good," Pooch said, rubbing his hand through his waves, thinking about the seven grand he just went out bad on. Easing the switch blade from his pocket, he jammed the knife in the man's throat as the other three men jumped back in shock. Pooch repeatedly stabbed him all over his body until he was covered in blood. He pulled the money out of his pocket and picked up the remaining bills that rested on the pavement. He put the knife back in his pocket and eased the 380 snapshots off his waist. "You pussies got three seconds to empty your pockets and take off running."

24

The men began emptying their pockets, dropping their valuables and followed suit with running behind each other. Pooch aimed his gun, letting off round after round.

Poc! Poc! Poc! Poc! Poc! Poc! Poc! The small handgun clapped, killing all three men. The two women across the street watched in horror as Pooch gathered up the money and looked at them.

"What y'all bitches staring at? Damn," Pooch said as he started jogging down the sidewalk. When he got to the end of the street, he made his way behind the corner store and jumped the fence, heading towards the Crown Heights apartments.

Walking through the bushes, his phone vibrated. He pulled it out, looking down at the message that sat on the screen. *"I'm on the way,"* he replied on the phone as he continued towards Flatbush and Fulton.

***

Ghost stepped out of his car, listening to his phone ring from Tiffany for the sixth time. He ignored the call as he grabbed the duffel bag and headed to the motel room he rented. Sticking the keycard in the slot, he looked both ways before he stepped in and closed the door. After sliding the bag under the bed, he checked the room thoroughly and sat in the fold out chair by the window. He thought about the horror that Erica could be going through as she sat in the hands of complete strangers.

The guilt ran through his head of all the curses and threats he was delivering to her a month back. The only thing that stuck in his brain was getting his child's mother back into his possession. He knew that he needed a team, and he also knew that the two hundred keys were the missing piece to even seeing Erica's face again.

Leaning back, he wiped the small tear from his eye, trying not to show any emotions. His heart was so cold. The ways of his lifestyle had his mind lost in a world of complete destruction. He was living the life of a person that existed inside of his mind. He always grasped a chance to show his love to Tiffany and Erica, and never held his end to either. The thoughts of his secrets really made him feel that he was the cause of the new demise landing on his head and family.

He picked up his phone and dialed Gunz's number and listened for an answer.

"Whoa, who dis?" Gunz spoke through the phone loudly.

"Ghost. I need to meet up with you and get your help with something."

"Bro, the last time I heard from you, all of y'all disappeared off the face of the earth. You know if you need me I'll gladly pull up," Gunz said, raising out of his bed.

"I need you to ride with me somewhere. Meet me at the Travel Lodge on Fulton Industrial. I'll be there in two hours," Ghost said, lighting the cigarette in front of him.

"I got you, Don. That's on the ten. I'm getting up right now."

"Two love." Ghost hung up the phone.

After he finished with his smoke break, he loaded his two guns back up and headed out of the room to Campbellton Road.

***

It had been over two hours since the incident with him and Ghost. The situation started to grow worse in D-Lo's mind as he mashed the gas down the expressway, ninety miles per hour. Suave sat in silence as he watched his friend go through his emotions. He knew that he and Ghost were official businessmen when it came down to the street shit. But their family was a lot more complicated and hard to understand than most people knew. It was all because of their family why Ghost was seeing everything crumble down and crash. But instead of helping each other through the small cracks, they were gunning at each other's throat all over a mishap. He didn't understand it at all, but his job was never made for understanding. Only loyalty and dirt naps. So, he just remained quiet until D-Lo made his next move.

"I gotta find out exactly where he is because Atlanta is too hot right now with our faces. If the wrong motherfucker sees us, we're done," D-Lo said, not paying attention to the black Yukon truck that followed them closely.

"Ghost is hell but I know he didn't want to truly hurt you, don. He's in his emotions right now about Erica and it's hard for him to be easy when he knows that his baby mother might not make it back after he worked so hard to end what you all were already going through."

"You're right. Things have been a little shaky around for the past few months. But I've never turned on him. I've sat back and watched relative after relative die, and I'm still standing here until it's all done. Without our loyalty, we have nothing. It's been me and my little brother since we were kids, and I've held my spot as his friend and closest family when no one else would."

"And he needs you even more now. Ghost isn't gonna just sit back and watch Erica die, no matter what she could have done. His mind is already set that he will die if that's what it takes for her to make it back home," Suave replied, looking over at D-Lo.

"And if it takes me to die with him then that's what I'm prepared to do. It's always OSA Gang and Mob life with me and I'm riding with my brother until a lucky mother-fucker send us to our maker."

"And you know my gun never runs out. I'm with you every step of the way. Especially if it has anything to do with a lil' killing," Suave said, looking out his window.

"As soon as we find him, the quicker we can get Erica back from these people and get the fuck out of the states." D-Lo spoke with a slight attitude.

Ghost pulled his whip inside the Venetian Hills apartments and made the first left, parking his car. Grabbing his gun, he took the keys out of the ignition and hopped out. He looked at the civilians who roamed the parking lot as he crossed the small bridge leading to the back of the apartments.

Knock, knock. Ghost tapped on the door twice, waiting on an answer.

"Whoa, who is it?" the deep voice asked from the other side of the door.

"Open it up and see," Ghost replied with his hands in his pockets.

The door began to rattle from the chains being released and opened. The man stared at Ghost hard before he leaped forward, grabbing him in a brotherly hug.

"Ghost! What the fuck is up, my boy?" Mark greeted him with a happy expression.

"Shit. Us as usual. You mind if I step in and holla at you for a second?" Ghost asked with a blank expression.

"Hell yeah, come in my nigga." Mark stepped aside, letting him slide in the house, locking the door back. He turned around and faced Ghost as he sat on the end of the

28

sofa chair. "What's been good with ya', homie? I ain't heard from you since you left Rice Street." Mark walked over to the small mini bar grabbing his Absolute.

"I been on the move lately. For some reason, we can't seem to stay in one spot. I came to offer you a proposition," Ghost said, looking him in the eyes.

"Look, bro, you my boy and all, but with all due respect, I haven't seen you in months and you appear out of nowhere. Is everything good?" Mark folded his arms.

"Everything mafioso, I just got a lot of different missions on my hand and I need some loyal niggas."

Mark took the Newport from behind his ear and lit it up as he took a deep breath. "What is it that you need me to do?"

"I need you to ride with me and not freeze up. I need bricks and I need 'em fast. You know I'm going to fill you in on what's going on, but there's a mean check in it for you, if you're interested."

Mark shook his head, understanding every word as he took another swig of his cup. "When does this shit get started, my nigga?"

"As soon as we walk out of this door. I'm not going to lie and tell you that it isn't any fuckery going on in the streets. But that money don't stop for no problem or wait for no nigga. So really, I'm asking you for a favor. Help me run this shit up and I'ma make sure you straight."

"What the hell we waiting on then?"

Ghost smiled with a devilish look as he got up and headed out the door with Mark on his heels. The city streets of Atlanta were about to come alive again until Ghost got what he needed. No one in his line of sight was safe.

Lockz sat in the apartment having a conversation with Dev when a knock on the door interrupted him mid-sentence. He grabbed the 223 rifle off the couch and looked out the peephole. Sliding the chain off the latch, he opened the door letting Pooch over the threshold.

"What's crackin' with you cripping ass niggas?" Pooch asked, acknowledging his cousin Dev with a smile.

"What ain't crackin' with us, B? Grape Street C's and a whole bunch of these," Dev replied, showing him a handful of Zanny bars.

Pooch grabbed a pill out of his hand before he sat on the opposite couch.

"Check this, right. I need you both to head to Atlanta. I don't want you to kill this nigga, son. It's a lot of paper and work on the line for this shit, so if we can pull this off, we can migrate to another borough."

"So, what the fuck you want us to do with the nigga? Have lunch with him?" Pooch asked, looking funny.

"No, jackass, I want you two to lay on his ass if he ain't doing what he supposed to on handling this debt. Y'all can wash that nigga whole fam, cuz. If he does what needs to be done, then y'all can leave him be and come back to the Big Apple and enjoy y'all paper," Lockz said, staring at both men.

Dev popped a Zanny and washed it down with the last of his Sprite soda. "When do we gotta leave?"

"Tonight. It's a fourteen-hour drive so I hope one of you niggas ready to stay up."

"Who the hell finna drive for fourteen hours and we can just get on a plane, Lockz?" Pooch butted in quickly.

"I'll drive," Dev answered, ready to get the movement in motion.

"Good. I'ma let you boys know what the fuck is crackin' with this busta ass nigga's address and phone number when y'all get close enough. It's not simple. This nigga ain't sweet. He's killing his own family so y'all got to be cautious."

"You can be tough and still get plated, my man. It's about the first one who draws down," Pooch spoke, tapping the handle of his strap.

Dev shook his head silently as he stood up. "Whatever you need us to do will get handled. Until then, I'ma fuck a couple of these niggas bitch's and wait for your call."

"Just stay out of sight and keep your eyes open for any bullshit. I'ma call the boss man and let him know shit is already in play. Crip easy and bang greasy."

Dev nodded as he headed for the door with Pooch following behind.

In the back of Lockz's mind he prayed that the two goons he chose could pull off the job. He knew that coming down to another killer's territory was dangerous and absurd. But the four million dollars he was promised from his connect was the major pay day he needed to be the King of Brooklyn once again.

Cat walked out of the bedroom and stared at Lockz as he sat deep in thought. "Are you okay, Daddy?"

The smell of her honey vanilla perfume invaded his nostrils as he looked up. Her Versace nightgown sat open, exposing her perfectly waxed pussy. Dev looked at her and flashed a small smile. "Get your ass over here, ma."

Cat slowly dropped her silky gown to the floor and walked over to Lockz, getting on her knees. She kissed his lips and began to unbutton his jeans, releasing his rod from his boxers. "Can mama have a lil' taste?" she asked, rubbing up and down his rising shaft.

"Stop playing with me and suck that dick."

Lockz's words made her pussy tingle harder as she took him in her mouth. She began to slowly massage her hands around his dick in a circular motion and she sucked him greedily. While she took him onto a blissful state of mind, he still wondered hard about his situation at hand. It was out of the ordinary for his boss to give him work that was out of state. He knew that his two young'ins were official, but neither one ever played in Atlanta. He knew that the ball game was in Ghost's advantage. But if Ghost ever wanted to see his bitch again, Lockz would make sure that he didn't if the wrong action was made.

He quickly tossed the thought out of his mind as his hand grabbed the back of Cat's head, gagging her for a few seconds.

"Mmm! It tastes so good, baby," Cat moaned, tapping his monster across her lips and tongue.

Cat was an ex-stripper-turned-housewife, thanks to Lockz. The mystery on how they met was barely told, but was known to everyone in their circle. She was shot three times by her ex-boyfriend in a strip club parking lot and left for dead. The long scar that ran down her neck told you that the beautiful tatted redbone had a rough past. Lockz washed the memory from his brain and laid his head back as Cat climbed on top of him.

Chapter 3

New York, NY

Pauly sat inside Patsy's Italian restaurant on W. 56th St. As usual he took his spot at the back table by the steps that led to the upper deck. He sat quietly with an expensive Cuban cigar burning in his hand as he read the New York Times newspaper. The female waitress arrived at the table with his meal and drink just as his cell phone vibrated.

"Order up, sir. Fried oregano fish with orange slices, celery and a side of tomato basil soup."

Pauly gave a small head nod and slid a hundred-dollar bill across the table to her hand.

"Thank you, sir, enjoy your meal," the waitress said, grabbing the money and walking off.

Pauly's bodyguard Tony sat at the middle table observing the movement inside the four-star eatery. After seeing the female waitress walk off, he got out of his chair and headed over to the boss' section.

"I don't think we are making the right choice on sending those idiots down there, Pauly. I think we should just have him whacked and show these fucking monkeys we're not playing," Tony said, heated that Lockz was headed to complete his mission.

"Patience is the way to any successful outcome. You've been out of commission, Tony. Lockz is the only key I can use at this time. You're a knight, not a pawn, son."

Tony watched as Pauly paused his speech to sip his drink. "To be honest, Pauly, if they're pawns, then I have to be a king to these imbeciles."

"You're not a king. I'm the king!"

"Come on, Pauly, you know I didn't mean it like that," Tony said, looking at his boss' cold stare.

"Loyalty plays a position in this form of business. We make choices to be the best, not the weakest. The reason you're sitting at this table with me is because you play an important part of this game. We're good guys and I'm the king of the chess board. If we kill this bastard that means the debt is unsealed. So, you explain to me what is the gain out of this action on whacking him?"

Tony sat back and gathered his thoughts before he spoke. "I'm just more of an illustrious person, Pauly. I'm more eminent, and these fucking pricks we have on our side are just a drag rope that's holding us back. We need men down there ASAP, Pauly. You've been sitting back waiting on this debt for over twenty years. I mean come on, boss. Don't you think it's time to just end this little problem?"

Pauly looked at Tony awkwardly as he fired up his cigar again. "Stop being so dramatic. Everyone down to the sixth generation will pay about the disrespect Jesus has brought upon me. No man, woman or child is exempt. If I let you go and kill this man right now, the only thing you would come back with is blood on your hands. So, what did you accomplish by taking a life? Did you get the money? Did you get my two hundred kilos of cocaine back?" Pauly sat in silence as he waited for an answer. "I take your quietness as an understanding. Make him pay his fees and kill everyone after. Send someone to kill a child or something. That should get his attention."

Tony held in his anger as he shook his head and got up to walk away from the table.

In Pauly's head, the situation was already handled. Ghost would either pay the ransom, or his family would suffer a horrible fate. It was rules to how every game was specifically played, and when that code was broken, the reaction was there to catch the mistake. After Pauly finished his cigar, looking out the glass window, he left a generous tip on the table as he got up and headed towards the front door.

It was six thirty in the evening when Ghost pulled his whip inside of the travel lodge efficiency. He drove to the middle of the parking lot and parked his car next to Gunz's white Impala. The travel lodge hotel was known to be a death trap at times. It was a heavy prostitution and crack area that sat on the busy strip of Fulton Industrial Boulevard.

Mark kept his eyes trained on the men who started to gather at the second-floor's rail. He knew that the travel lodge wasn't the place to come for a sweet lick. But he also knew that he was killing anyone who thought about getting in the way.

Gunz stepped out of his whip and got inside the backseat of Ghost's Challenger. "So, what the fuck mobbing? What we gotta do?" he asked Ghost.

"We're about to go in here, take these bricks and get him to tell us his connections, so we can do the same with him."

"That's cool, but the dude right there in the red shirt, he got like a Glock nine on his hip. The one in the white has a black three-fifty-seven that's sitting on the floor in front of him, and the rest of them niggas there just to make it seem like they're all real killers."

"How long have you been sitting here?"

Gunz shrugged his shoulders trying to think of an accurate estimate. "About twenty-five minutes. After they saw my car pull up, they began to crowd around like they were having a group meeting or some shit."

"They know what we're about to do. I think we should just go ahead and take care of our business before they start to call more than we can handle," Mark butted in, keeping his eyes on the crowd.

Gunz looked at Ghost, then back over at Mark with a stale face. "Who the fuck are you?"

Mark turned his head toward the backseat, looking at Gunz. "I was just about to ask you the same thing."

"Hey, cut that shit. Is y'all niggas ready?" Ghost asked interfering with the fake ass background check.

"I'm ready," Mark said, looking back and forth between both men.

Ghost was the first person to lead as he opened the car door, stepping out. Gunz and Mark followed his lead, doing the same as they headed around to room 201. Ghost eyed the men from the top rail as they began making their way to the steps to come down.

"Here they come, fellas. Don't kill them if we ain't got to," Ghost whispered as the four men came around the corner, meeting them at the curve of the breezeway.

"Can we help you niggas with something?" One of the four men asked.

Mark wasted no time pulling his pistol and striking the man in the face.

"Whoa, now," Ghost said as he and Gunz drew down on the other three men who looked on in shock.

Mark hit the man over nine times until he laid unconscious on the pavement. He removed the man's pistol from his waist and leveled them at the three men.

"I 'preciate that," Gunz said to the man in the white tee as he removed his three-fifty-seven from his hip.

"Y'all go ahead. I got these pussy ass niggas," Mark said, holding all the men at gunpoint.

"You sure?" Ghost asked cautiously.

"You could have already been back by now, my nigga," he replied, ready to end things as smoothly as possible. The area was hot and any shots would lead to police flooding the area of the open hotel.

Ghost smiled as he made his way around the corner with Gunz on his heels. Standing on the side of the room, he knocked lightly three times and waited for an answer

"Yo, who is it?" Dwight asked, trying to look through the peephole of the door.

"I'm from room one thirty-six, my nigga. I was just looking for some gas, my boy," Gunz spoke with a fake southern accent.

Gunz listened to the locks as they shifted. When the door cracked just an inch, he raised his foot, kicking it completely open. The metal collided with Dwight's head, sending him to the floor as Ghost and Gunz made their way in.

"Dwight, Dwight," Ghost said as he shut the room door behind them.

"Ghost," he replied with a look of terror in his eyes. "I thought you were dead, bro. What's good?" Dwight asked as if he didn't have a gun pointed at the top of his head.

"Bricks? Where are they?"

"Look, Ghost, I know I owe you a little paper from a lil' while back. I'ma handle that, man, I promise. I can't take a loss right now, big dog."

Gunz slapped Dwight in his face with the butt of the gun, making him hold his eye and jaw.

"Ahh! Oh fuck, it's under the bed! It's under the bed," he screamed, kicking his feet from the pain.

Gunz walked over to the bed and got on his knees, pulling the gray Nike bag from underneath as Ghost watched Dwight pathetically.

"You should have paid me my money, Dwight."

"I thought you were fucking dead, man. You've been gone almost a year, Ghost. How was I supposed to know you were going to pop back up looking for thirty grand off two bricks you fronted me after you disappeared?"

"You don't spend a man's money if you know that there is a debt you owe, Dwight. It was great meeting you again, tho'," Ghost said, heading for the door.

Gunz looked at Dwight with an "I don't give a fuck" expression and leaned down beside him.

"You're lucky I'm in a good mood today, faggot. It woulda been a pleasure to murder yo' stupid ass." He laughed and made his way out of the room.

Coming back around the corner, Mark still held the men at gunpoint as they faced the wall.

"We got what we came for, Don. Let's get the fuck outta here," Ghost said, tapping Mark's shoulder.

Mark started to back away as he kept his aim leveled at the four men. "Y'all pussy ass niggas have a good day," he said with a smile as he jumped in the car with Ghost and Gunz to pull off.

Ghost hit the expressway thinking about their next target as he headed back to his motel room.

***

D-Lo paced the crib, thinking of what to do next. Suave sat back quietly as he watched his friend stress about the annoying issue.

"Everything's gonna be aight, Lo. We just gotta think this shit through. It's not many people who know we're back in this city. I say let's go out and make this shit happen. We ain't got too many options. I know a nigga out in Jack City named Lil' Bentley. He's known to keep a ten or fifteen on him in his spot all the time. He's cool, but he's a rat, so really that's a free meal."

"That's cool, Don, but we far off from two hundred keys. It's a start, and we need everything we can put our hands on. I'm just trying to think of a bigger play."

D-Lo's phone began to ring loudly as it sat on the table. He quickly answered the phone without looking, feeling that it was Ghost.

"Whoa, bruh?" D-Lo spoke through the receiver.

"Whoa, nigga, what the fuck mobbing?"

"Who the fuck is this?" D-Lo asked, not recognizing the voice.

"This Don Smashiano."

"Man, what the fuck mobbing, Don? How the hell you get my number?"

"Come on Lo, it's the mobb, bro. I got a lil' something in play that you might need."

"Talk to me, bro, what's good?" D-Lo replied, listening closely.

"I heard y'all got a little situation on ya' hands and y'all need some weight. Word on the street is Ghost mixed himself in a little jam with some people."

"Yeah, Don, it's a lot going on right now. Shit is ugly and whoever is speaking on this shit needs to stay quiet before they come up missing."

"Trust me, bro, it's nothing like that. You know Ghost is the talk of the town. Anyway, I got some niggas out here in Regency Park and they're willing to do a little business with y'all on the strength of your reputation in this city."

"What are they talking about?"

"They got birds going for thirty a piece. I let them know you boys needed as much work as possible. They were a little skeptical at first, but on the strength of y'all's niggas press game they willing to front y'all the weight on one circumstance."

"And what's that?" D-Lo asked, feeling that they hit the jackpot.

"Y'all gotta pull up on them. But they don't want Ghost around. They only want to do business with you."

"What type of shit is that? I don't even know these niggas. Me and my brother are a team. It's no such thing as doing business without him," D-Lo said, feeling like it could be a set-up.

"Don, they don't trust Ghost. Do you know they found Red dead in his house like three hours ago? Word is that bro just did that. He hasn't even been back to the city two weeks and he just murdered a nigga who supplied half of the A. Niggas are spooked, bro. Everybody is sitting back wondering who is next and these niggas here ain't trying to be on that list.

D-Lo rubbed his hands through his dreads from what Smashiano told him. He knew Ghost was mad and was on the lurk for the weight, but he didn't think he would go as far killing his own connect.

"Where do they wanna meet at?" He asked, feeling this may be his only chance of making something happen.

"Meet me in the plaza in front of the apartments. I set everything up off my reputation with this man. Please bro, do not kill these people," Smashiano said, knowing the way he and Ghost rocked.

"Listen, bro, I'm bringing my shooter with me for safety purposes. Ain't nothing finna go down as long as they do straight up business."

"Nothing left to be said, Don. Meet over this way in about an hour. I'll be waiting for you."

"Two love."

"Two many, bro," Smashiano said, hanging up the line.

"I think we might've just found our way and I don't even think we gotta kill nobody to get it."

"What's the plan?" Suave asked, leaning off the couch.

"We gotta take a trip to Regency Park."

"Do I need to come with you?" Michael asked, sitting in the corner listening to his son.

"Naw, Pop. I don't need you being seen right now. I know you wanna help, but it's better if we move a lil' silent on this problem right now. You haven't been around in twenty years. It's better if you stay low and ducked off until we leave Atlanta."

Micheal shook his head, standing up. "Listen I know you feel that you guys have all of this under control, and things will work out perfectly. The time I've been away has caused torment in this family. I waited long for the day that I will meet back up with my children. It's only so long that I can keep sitting back, watching you all destroy your-selves. You need to let me help guide us the right way be-fore it gets worst."

"He's right bro. Do you really feel like we not finna have to murder anyone of these stupid ass niggas, D-Lo? You know I'm always down for whatever, but I don't like surprises."

D-Lo thought hard before he answered. In a certain way, Suave was right. They were at war with a lot of dif-ferent people and anyone could have a plot to set them up. "Dad, I feel you, but trust me on this. Sauve, if you feel anything stupid, kill everyone in that bitch!"

41

"That sounds like fun," Suave said as he and D-Lo headed out of the door.

Chapter 4

Sitting in the dark small room, Erica jumped out of her sleep as if she had a nightmare. The shackles around her ankles and chains around her wrists let it be known that it was well much reality. The chains were connected to a concrete wall, her feet were latched on to a small loop on the floor, and a small camera sat above the door directly at her face, watching every move she made. Erica looked around at the brown solid painted walls. Her agent instincts started to kick in as she began to plot on any way she could make it out of wherever she was. The door to the room opened, startling her. She slid her back to the concrete as the tall, Black male stepped in and closed the door.

He stood quietly in the center of the room and thought hard before he spoke. "Are you hungry?"

She held her stare with him without blinking, but still didn't say a word.

Walking over to her, he grabbed one of her handcuffed wrists as he looked down. "If you do anything stupid to make me kill you, then it's your fault." He placed the key inside the lock and unlatched her hand. "I'ma leave the other one on just in case you try to do too much and start fucking with shit." The man ranted as he dropped a bag full of French fries beside her.

He pulled a bottle of Dasani water from his pocket and tossed it in her lap. As the man walked back out, she looked around nervously at anything she could use to help her. But it was no hope. The handcuffs were sealed into the concrete. She knew whoever had her was watching. But that bad feeling in her heart said that she wouldn't make it out of the cold room alive.

Tiffany opened her eyes from the light sleep she was in. Bernard and Laylah slept peacefully on the side of her, and Mariah sat at the end of the bed, watching the flat screen on the wall.

"Mommy. I'm hungry!"

Tiffany sat up, rubbing her eyes and climbed out of bed. "I got you, baby girl, let me go fix you something." Grabbing her pants, she slid them on before she walked in the living room.

Michael sat by the window, looking out of the thin blinds.

"Where is D-Lo and Suave?" Tiffany asked, seeing him alone in the house.

"They headed out, looking for Chance. I think D'Angelo has probably found another way to gather some keys from someone. He told me to lay low, so I stayed back in hopes that I would catch Chance coming through."

"Ghost used to always tell me you were dead. How did you just end up finding him before he left California?" Tiffany asked, wanting to know some answers.

"I thought I was dead. Every day I woke up in the same room, I told myself that it was just a dream. I told myself that it was no way I was still alive. I thought about my boys every day that I sat in that tank. You tell me how would you feel if you spent twenty years inside a box? Never seeing a face, never hearing a voice. I trained my mind when I was down in that hole. I knew in my heart that it was possibly gonna be my graveyard. I was gone so long that my son grew into a man and killed my father right above my head. My son, who I haven't laid eyes on in all these years, literally murdered my father twenty minutes before my sister set me free. Do you know how that feels?" Michael asked, looking deeply into her eyes.

"How are we supposed to end this with these people? Ever since I've been around this family, drama and secrets have torn it down more and more. We have no structure or understanding. We're at war right now with other outsiders because your father couldn't take the time to accept his own grandkids. He couldn't even be a supporting father and stand by his own son's side."

Michael shook his head knowing that Tiffany was spilling the truth. All of this was happening because Jesus wanted to be an asshole without helping to support his grandkids. The painful words that his father spoke to him ran through his head as he sat in deep thought.

"You made your bed and you will have to lay in it." Jesus told him after finding out about the three kids he had in Atlanta.

"It was about more than just the kids, wasn't it?" Tiffany asked, sensing he wanted to say something.

"My father was mad that I got two Black women pregnant, more than anything. His hate for Black women came after my brother deceived him with my mother."

"What? How is something like that possible? I thought you and your sister was Jesus's only children."

"My older brother would be forty-seven now if he was still here with us."

Tiffany looked at him with a stone face in confusion. "Jesus killed your brother?"

"My half-brother. Phillipe was full Spanish; he rarely came around me and Eva. When he did decide to pop up, he and my father could never get along. For some reason, my mom enjoyed when he came over. My father knew that Phillipe was a little past his age when it came to being his oldest son. One day, he came in the house and caught my brother on top of my mother in his bed. His brain couldn't handle the situation and he sliced Phillipe's throat with a knife in that room. I stood downstairs and watched my mother being dragged out the house by Jesus. He put her in the car and drove off, leaving me and my sister there for hours. When he returned, he was alone and he told us to grab our things. He made it clear that if we ever mentioned anything about what we saw, he would make sure our bodies were buried right beside theirs."

"Your mother was a Black woman?"

"One hundred percent, and my dad couldn't accept that his son went behind him and slept with his wife. Jesus' hate for Black people grew tremendously. He even started to use me as if I wasn't his son. Being called a half-breed by your own father will show you there's no love from really anyone. I was brought into this family business at the age of fourteen for one reason. Killing."

"You mean in context as in hitman?"

"Yes. I was my father's personal bodyguard. If he ever had any problem in state or out, I was the one to go and handle it. When I turned sixteen, I moved to Atlanta on my own and stationed myself. Upon my stay, I ended up getting two different Black women pregnant. I wanted to live my own life, but telling him that I had children on the way was something that wasn't gonna happen. I continued to fly to California and handle my issues or whatever I was assigned to do. And one day I just came out and told him."

"And what did he say?"

"He told me to get out of his house. He told me I wouldn't receive another dime from him. He said it wasn't any more space in the Ramirez family for me, so I left. The hurt in my heart is what triggered me to do the things I did. I heard about a transaction that was set to go down that same night between him and the Italians. It wasn't a major priority to me, but hearing fifty million is what stopped me in my tracks. Jesus was an unforgiveable person. I knew he could never let me back in. Working for the family business was the only thing I had left to feed myself. When he cut me off from that, he brought out the animal I contained for so long. I popped up in the middle of the transaction deal the same night. I murdered every man that stood in the parking lot. I took the fifty million dollars and headed to Atlanta. Before I could make it to my kids, I was knocked unconscious after I buried the money. That was the last thing I remembered before I was let out of that entrapment twenty years later."

"Does Ghost know about any of this?"

"I think it's best if he doesn't," Michael replied quickly.

"We have to end this. Things are more twisted than I expected. If we don't help Ghost, he's going to crash out about this situation. Not only is he my friend, he's my husband in my eyes. I don't care if I have to kill everyone who gets in the way."

"The only person who has to agree is Chance. We don't wanna do anything that would make him feel we could put Erica in more jeopardy. We have to dig up this money. Pauly is not going to touch her and blow any chance of him receiving his payment. Playing with him is not just a walk in the park."

"And neither is over here. I've busted my ass getting to the top of this food chain by killing bitches like Pauly all the time. The time to stop playing is over. We've wasted enough time hurting the people close to us instead of the real enemies."

"I agree with you," Michael said, rubbing his temples to relieve the pressure.

"I think we need to hurry up and do something before reality sets in that we actually might not get her back," Tiffany said, walking off into the kitchen.

Michael shook his head, knowing her words were like the truth from God. He knew that Pauly was a big problem, and if it took him to bring the animal out and help his son, then that's exactly what it was going to be.

Ghost, Mark and Gunz made their way to the entrance of the hotel. Ghost drove through the gate and parked in front of his room. Mark grabbed the Nike duffle as all the men got out of the car and headed inside.

"What's next?" Gunz asked as they all gathered around the table, pouring out the contents in the bag.

"The same as usual. I really fuck with ya'll boys, so I gotta put you on the game. It's not really about the paper flow. I have enough to buy whatever I need, times a hundred. The problem is the connect on this weight. They kidnapped Erica. My grandfather owed these people two hundred keys of cocaine and they ain't considering taking the paper in replacement."

"They kidnapped who?" Gunz asked with all seriousness.

"Erica."

"Why you ain't been told us this, my nigga? Where is she?" Mark asked, feeling bad in his heart for Ghost's woman.

"She's in New York. The Italians got her."

"Shit." Mark rubbed his hands through his head. "That's a totally different ball game, Ghost. Those folks ain't bullshitting."

"How would we even know if she's still alive?" Gunz chimed in.

"Whoever these guys think they are, they really aren't. If it was me who had the ball in my court, I would have killed the girl off-top just to let you know I meant business. The way they confronted me after they took her was some pussy shit. A nigga from up top claimed to work for him but was very blunt and discreet. He told me if I wanted Erica back, to get the bricks and the fifty million my pop repo'd from him twenty years back."

Gunz rubbed his finger inside of his ear as if he'd just been struck with a gun. "Did you just say fifty million, Don?"

Ghost nodded, confirming Gunz's question.

"Not to make you psych out or nothing, bro. Do you even think she's still alive?" Mark replied, looking him in the eyes.   Just thinking about it made him slightly blackout. His pupils began to get big as he took a deep breath. Balling up his fists, he looked at them with a hurt expression.

"I know she's alive. Erica is a woman, but she's smart. She's a fucking fed."

"She's what? We can't be talking about the sweet Erica that I met months and months ago. She's Twelve?"

"She *was* a fed. They tried to make her turn me in for questioning and she denied them. She even went as far as running with me. I owe her my loyalty. She's not just my girl bro, she's my child's mother, and the only way I'm going to get her back is if I get some help."

"Ghost, fifty million and two hundred keys isn't something that we can just stumble up on. It'll take forever to try and get that much paper and dope." Gunz spoke the truth.

"The fifty isn't the problem. We have access to the money. It's the bricks that's gonna be the trouble. We haven't been in Atlanta in almost nine months. Everybody has been dragging our name through the dirt. So, no one really wants to do business with us."

"So why don't we just go and get her ourselves? The longer we wait is more worst on us then it is on them."

"That's my plan. In order for it to work, I have to get this ransom. It's a fifty-fifty chance that they keep their word and let her go. I don't wanna spook these people and make them kill her."

"How many keys do we already have?" Gunz asked, looking at the thirteen bricks on the table.

"We have twenty-one, plus this sixteen on the table. If we split it down the middle, it's like twelve or twelve a piece for us." Ghost said, realizing it wasn't enough.

"Keep all them bitches, bro. We need to get your woman back. We will eat when the chance comes." Mark said, pushing the weight towards him.

"How about this," Ghost said, pushing all the money towards them.

"What do you want us to do with this?"

"It's for y'all to split. Whenever we strike for the paper, I'll let you boys divide that and I'll keep collecting the weight to put towards Erica."

Mark flashed a slight smile, dapping Ghost up. "That's real love, my boy."

"It's all family love with y'all two, bro. When this is over, it's gonna be more where that came from."

"So, what are we gonna do now?"

"We're about to rape the city for whatever we can. After we get enough to get Erica back, we're gonna take a trip to New York and have us a little fun up there. Tomorrow we headed back to Campbellton. I got something extra sweet lined up." Ghost said in a death-like tone.

Ghost looked down at D-Lo's name flashing across the phone for the second time and ignored his call. All he could think about was Erica. Now that she was away from him, he literally started to see how important she was. Even though she kept a secret that destroyed half of their trust mark, he wasn't willing to let her go. He knew that it was no such thing as giving up on her. The smell of death rose through his nostrils as he envisioned throwing Pauly out of a ten-story window.

Chris Green

Chapter 5

D-Lo tried Ghost's phone for the last time as he pulled into the plaza next to Smashaino's Charger.

"Whoa," D-Lo said, rolling down the window as he blew out a cloud of smoke from the Moon Rock Kush.

"What's mobbing, bro? Look, just follow my lead and we about to make this shit happen as quickly as possible. I don't need y'all shooting niggas all in the head and sticking niggas and shit."

"Man, can we go ahead and handle this shit?" Suave asked.

Smashiano looked over at Suave and saw the fuckery written all over him. "Follow me," he said, slowly pulling out and heading up the hill inside the apartments.

D-Lo kept the whip close behind Smashiano as he made the first left, parking in front of the building. From the look of the six men that stood outside, they obviously didn't trust Smashiano's word that the good vibes were mutual. D-Lo and Suave put their straps on their hip before exiting the car and walked to the door of the apartment.

"Whoa, we here to see Blake." Smashiano said, leading in front of them.

"Who the fuck are you niggas?" The young'in asked aggressively, making the five other men gather around.

"Lower your voice, my nigga. I just told you we were here to see Blake."

Suave stared at the other five men coldly, waiting for them to reach for anything he could see, but D-Lo remained quiet.

Before the man could reply, the door came open and Blake stepped out, looking like he stayed in a mansion instead of a two-star apartment complex. "What's good fellas? Is everything straight?"

"Nah, my boy. Ya' country ass worker right here obviously don't know who we are. Is it time to handle business now?" D-Lo asked as all the workers looked dumbfounded.

"Of course. It's always time to do business, and don't mind Jaylen here. He takes his job to the extreme sometimes. Come in, gentlemen."

Blake stepped to the side, allowing Smashiano, D-Lo and Suave to enter the spot. Before he closed the door, he gave Jaylen a disappointing stare and headed to complete his mission.

"So, what's up? Talk to me." Blake said, grabbing four beers out the cooler, passing them around.

"You obviously heard because we're having this meeting right now. We need weight," D-Lo said, sliding the beer away from him.

"I understand that part. The question is how much?"

"I'll take all of it if it has the right ticket on it."

Blake smiled as he sipped his beer. "No disrespect, but you don't even know what I'm holding to say you will buy everything."

"Well, all you have to do is name your fucking price and we can get an understanding before it turns to morning." Suave said, starting to get impatient.

"Whoa, chill, bro. Look, Blake, can we just talk numbers and get this over with?" Smashiano asked, feeling the bullshit approaching.

Blake continued to stare at Suave with an insulted frown before he put his attention back to D-Lo. "My keys

54

go for thirty a piece. Depending on how many you purchase, I can knock a certain percentage off. I only serve one time out of a month, so whatever you're trying to do, has to be done now."

"I need two hundred keys. You think that's enough to handle?"

"Two hundred keys? Who the hell do you think I am, El Chapo?" Blake asked seriously.

D-Lo stared at him quietly, waiting for a direct answer to their problem.

Blake shook his head and walked to the back room. D-Lo and Suave looked at each other and over at Smashiano.

"Don't ask me, bro," he whispered, shrugging.

Blake re-entered the room with a huge black garbage bag and sat it on the table. "That's thirty-four right here. Uncut, straight clean. I'm doing this deal for Smashiano, but I'm letting y'all in for twenty a piece. On good peace with Ghost, I'll give 'em to you up front. That's six hundred and eighty thousand US dollars," Blake said, looking D-Lo in the eyes.

"What's the catch to this?"

"There is no catch. It's simple business. I respect y'all because of what you stand on. Y'all on some city shit. That's what I was birthed on. I look you in yo' face and I can see a real nigga. I can't do nothing but give the blessing and hope that you don't prove me wrong."

"If you've heard of us as you say, then you would know that our family isn't hurting for anything. We built most of these streets in this city from crumbs to blocks. I'll have your paper delivered to you by morning," D-Lo said, grabbing the garbage bag.

"Understood."

After shaking hands and sealing the deal, Blake walked the men back to their car.

"I'ma hit ya' line, Don," Smashiano said, jumping back in his whip.

D-Lo nodded and looked over at Blake. After throwing him a salute, he and Suave hopped in the whip and backed out.

"You sure these niggas ain't feds, bro?" Suave asked.

D-Lo looked over at Suave and cracked a smile. "Hell nah. Don is just plugged with a lot of different niggas." Suave continued to look in the rear-view mirror until they turned out of the complex.

"Yeah, that's all good, but I never seen a nigga that'll cough up off thirty-four bricks like it ain't shit without no paper in hand."

"It's a mutual understanding between boss niggas. Blake only heard of us from the streets. He knows we touch money that niggas would dream to have. He also knows that we've wacked niggas who everyone swear was untouchable. It's a reverse cycle. He's just showing us the love before the victims run out, which would place his name at the top of the list."

"Well, if niggas keep playing it safe like this, all we gotta do is take this weight and mobb easy. We should be able to get Erica back and get the fuck away from the A for good."

Stopping at the red light by Washington Road, D-Lo looked to his side at the beautiful woman who sat in the big Yukon truck next to them. "Hey, sweetie," he mouthed, waving a light hand at her.

Pulling her hair back in a ponytail, she looked over at him smiling. As the light turned green, she waved before making the left at the Rite Aid as D-Lo kept straight.

"Don, these bitches are so bad in the A. Sometimes, I don't even be wanting to leave this motherfucker," D-Lo said, thinking about the dime piece he just viewed. Making a quick stop, he pulled into the BP gas station, parking directly in front of the store. "You need anything out of here, bro?" D-Lo asked, opening his car door.

"Nah, I'm good, bro. Just grab me a Rello."

"I gotcha."

D-Lo stepped out of the car and headed inside the store. As Suave sat dazed inside of his phone, the loud tire screeching caused him to look up quickly in the side view mirror. Seeing the Mexican jump out of the car eased his nerves, but the pistol he pulled out of his pants sent the radar through the roof. It was clear that he was on a mission as he made his way over to D-Lo's car. Suave cocked his pistol and eased down in the passenger seat. The Mexican instantly pulled the car door handle as he tried to look through D-Lo's tinted window.

Boom!

The glass from the window exploded as Suave pulled the trigger, sending a bullet flying through his brain. As his body hit the ground, two more Mexicans from the vehicle popped out as D-Lo came bursting out the store. Suave slid out the passenger side, cranking his gun. *Boc! Boc! Boc! Boc! Boc! Boc! Boc!* His glock erupted loudly as he popped from behind the car. D-Lo pulled his pistol from his waist with expertise and began to bust as the two other men returned fire.

"Punta motherfuckers," one Mexican yelled as he tried to shoot without looking. *Bloc! Bloc! Bloc! Bloc! Bloc! Bloc!*

The bullet that struck him at the top of his head made him drop his weapon and fall to the ground. D-Lo and

Suave bust their guns, making the second man climb in the car and skate off. The clinking of the bullets hitting the car door made the man panic as he swerved out into the middle of the street. The Marta bus that blindsided the car flipped it twice before it landed on the hood and slid a few feet across the street. D-Lo ran over to the car, jumping in, and did a full 360 out of the gas station's parking lot.

"What the fuck just happened?"

"I don't know. A fucking Mexican just pushed up on the car with a burner. He came out of nowhere," Suave replied, still gripping his burner as he looked back.

"A Mexican? We don't have any beef with no fucking Mexicans! We never even done any business with any."

D-Lo turned down a quick side street before smashing the pedal to the floor. After he ran the red light crossing over to Headland and Delowe Drive, he began to ease his foot up off the gas.

"The man you just shot, have you ever seen him before?"

"Yeah, I think I have," Suave said, thinking hard.

D-Lo looked over at him and back to the road. "Where?"

"I'm not a hundred percent sure, but I think I seen him walking out of Ghost's club one night when I pulled up to get Woodie."

"That could have been anybody, bro. That was in Cali. We're back in Atlanta."

Suave shook his head, thinking hard, trying to remember everything he could and it finally came to him. "That was the Mexican from California."

"How do you know that for sure?"

"Because he's the same Mexican that left out of the lot behind JL and Trouble the night they died."

D-Lo's face hardened from hearing his friend's name. "Are you serious?"

"I'm positive. It took a minute to hit me, but JL and Trouble walked directly past me. I asked where they were going and JL said they would be right back. As I kept walking towards the club, a Mexican brushed past me, moving awkwardly as fuck. He looked me directly in the eyes but kept it pushing like he was in a hurry. It was something about the way he looked at me. It was like he knew who I was or something."

"Shit," D-Lo said, pulling out his phone to call Ghost. He knew that if Suave's words were true, then it was more than just a family beef going on. It was someone literally on the hunt for them.

Chris Green

Chapter 6

Morning time just began to creep pass the windshield of the car. It was 6:45 in the morning and Dev's feet were extra tired from driving. An evil smile stretched across his face as he drove under the Atlanta City Limits expressway sign.

"Yo, cuz, wake up."

Pooch laid balled up in the passenger seat, sleep with a small container of orange juice tipping in his hand.

Blatt, Blatt.

Pooch jumped out of sleep hearing the blood sound ringing through his ears. "Man, stop fucking playing, Dev. You know I don't fuck with them folks."

"Nigga, you the one acting like you can't hear. Them bloods woulda been all on yo ass." Dev laughed at his own joke.

"Ha-Ha-Ha! Wassup, dumb ass nigga?"

"What you mean wassup? We here, dumb ass nigga."

Pooch took his feet off the dash and started to stare out of the glass. He looked back over at Dev with an ecstatic face. "This is Atlanta?"

"Nah, it's Atlantis, B."

Pooch burst out in laughter as he took in the different scenery. "I'm about to wreck this place. This shit looks too sweet, son."

"Yo, pause young'in. I know you ready to take flight down here and get straight to it, but you can't do that."

"I don't see why not. These niggas don't know us down here. I wanna light they ass for everything."

"And that's understood, but we not up top right now. We know our way around the Bronx, but this is a totally different atmosphere. These cats down here play grimy, and if we slip, we gone die down here."

"Man, look, We ain't been getting killed. I ain't none but eighteen and I got nine of 'em under my belt. If these cookie ass Atlanta niggas want some, B, waist these clowns and let's brush on. You act like you ain't murdered half of Flatbush and Utica Avenue, Dev."

"I never said that. It's just a certain way we gotta move. You know we gone get our feet wet and get this extra bread in this foreign ass state. We can even give a few of these bitches a dirt nap. Just remember we still got a job that we have to do. A job that's paying us a lot of cheese, cuz," Dev said, looking over at his cousin.

"Yeah, yeah, whatever. So, where the hell we going if we don't know nobody or our way around this mother-fucker?"

"I got a cousin who stay on Cleveland Avenue. That's where we gonna be staying while we down here. Wherever we go, we're just gonna have to use the GPS on my iPhone. That means no splitting up, Pooch. It's easy to get caught up in the wrong hood and get yo' ass killed. You need to lay low and just chill. No renegade shit. We gonna get us a lil' paper and handle this nigga. Once we done, we up outta here."

"Say less, cuz. I got you."

The words that Dev spoke went through one ear and out the other as Pooch thought about all the fuckery he was going to bring to Atlanta. Uptown niggas were a different breed, and with Dev or not, he was ready to set the standards.

Ghost cracked his eyes from the ringing of the loud hotel phone. He yawned, stretching his arms as he sat up on the side of the bed. Wiping his eyes clear, he picked up the phone with his other hand. "Whoa?"

"Bro, why aren't you picking up the phone?" D-Lo asked in a worried voice.

Ghost took a deep breath after hearing his brother. "I'm straight, man. I'm minding my own fucking business. How in the fuck did you even know I was here?"

"I'm still your fucking brother. Just because we get into a little dispute doesn't mean that I'ma leave yo' side, bro. We got a problem."

"Can't be more of a problem then what I got going on."

"Listen, Ghost. Someone is after us and I don't think they're tryna hide that they won't smoke. Do you remember Blake?"

Ghost's mind instantly clicked to a green light when he heard the name through the phone. "Hell yeah, I remember Blake. The brown skin, pretty boi ass nigga who had the weight in Camp Creek a while back. He got knocked for a body in 2012."

"Exactly. He beat that shit. The nigga is on the street right now as we speak."

"What? Where the fuck is he? That nigga is major strapped with the work. He might be our way."

"My point exactly. That's what I'm trying to tell you. Smashiano called me yesterday and told me the nigga had blocks for thirty a piece."

"Smashiano? I thought he was down the road."

"He's been out for about two months now. It kinda sounded suspect at first and I really wanted to get your input before I made a move."

"How da fuck does he know Blake?" Ghost asked, wondering what Smashiano had up his sleeve.

"I guess him and Blake know of each other. He called and told me Bro was willing to do business with us under one condition."

"And what's that?"

"He doesn't want you around when the exchange is being handled."

Ghost immediately took the remark as disrespect and started to blow. "What da fuck do you mean I can't be around when the business getting handled? It's my fucking paper!"

"Bro, the nigga is fucking spooked of you being around. He told me what you did to Red."

"I don't know what the fuck you're talking about. I can't help it that these niggas are pussies and scared. Matter fact, where is he? I'll just go and take all of that shit."

"It's too late. The shit is already gone."

"What do you mean it's already gone? You just said the nigga had birds for thirty a pop."

"Yeah he did. I went and picked the last thirty-four up last night when we met up."

"He sold you thirty-four bricks?" Ghost asked, thinking he may have misheard him.

"No, he fronted me thirty-four. I just took the authority to go ahead and pay him. We ain't never owed a nigga shit. He told me the only reason he was giving them to me up front is to make peace with you because he knew we needed them ASAP."

"It's a start. I got thirty-seven, so with yours in all we have seventy-one. It's still not enough to get her back. I'm not stopping until I get the rest of those birds."

"I'm with you, bro, but that's not really the problem."

"What do you mean?" Ghost asked, sliding his shirt on.

"After me and Suave left Blake's spot, we had a run in with some dudes at a gas station."

"It's probably some niggas we robbed a while back or something. You know how that shit go. We can't expect niggas not to notice us the whole time we down here."

"Ghost, it was two Mexicans."

"What? We don't got no fucking problems with no Mexicans. You might just be trippin'."

"Nah, I'm far from trippin. Suave told me he seen the same Mexican somewhere before that incident. At first, I thought he was losing it, but after his mind got right and he remembered where he saw him, he clarified the whole situation."

"So where does he remember this motherfucker from?"

"From your club in LA. Suave say he saw that pussy leave out the same night JL and Trouble got killed. He said he was positive."

Hearing D-Lo mention the strip club made Ghost's heart skip a beat. JL and Trouble's names instantly began to run through his brain as he tried to think a little harder.

"Do you think they worked for Jesus?" D-Lo questioned, trying to see if his brother felt the same.

"I wouldn't doubt it, but Jesus is dead, bro. How much sense does it make to keep chasing someone who just murdered your boss? You wouldn't even know where to start from. We left that shit in Cali, so how in the fuck would they know we're in Atlanta, because a dead man can't talk."

"My point exactly. It's something going on that we can't see, bro. We already have a lot on our plate with these slimy ass Italians. I feel like we need to relocate. We need to keep a low profile on Pop, Tiffany and the kids until we got enough weight to get Erica back."

"I'm on a mission and I'm not stopping. We need a hundred and twenty-nine more, and we're nowhere near that. I've been playing it cool, but I'm about to say fuck trying to move silent and let this shit loose. I don't think we got too much time left."

D-Lo sat back and felt his brother's pain. Erica was their family. Not only that, she birthed his nephew. He could only imagine what she was really going through while being away from her son and the entire family. "I know this is a fucked up situation, but I'm gonna be right here until we walk out with her. I'm sorry that shit happened like that between me and you yesterday, lil' bro. I don't never want you to think that I'm against you."

"I ain't worried about you being against me, nigga. The next time you hit me in my shit like that, I'ma shoot ya ass fo' real," Ghost said.

D-Lo couldn't help but to laugh. "Look, me and Suave got another play for today on some more work. We gonna stay on it until we get whatever we need."

"Understood. I'm on the same page. Everything I make happen, I'll pull up on you and let y'all know. Obviously, you know what hotel I'm at so I'ma need you to come pick this shit up. It's gonna be under the bed and I'ma leave a key card under the mat outside."

"I got you, bro. I'll head over that way in a second."

"Cool. Who the fuck told you where I was, nigga?" Ghost asked, still wondering.

"Come on, bro. You know Gunz love me just as much as he fucks with you," D-Lo said, hanging up the phone.

Ghost placed the phone back on the hook and grabbed his cell phone off the night stand. Dialing Shadow's number, he placed the line up to his ear waiting for an answer.

"What's good, folk?"

"Broooo, what the fuck mobbing, my dude?"

"The usual; trying to fuck my way through this world to a better life. Have you heard anything else about Erica?"

"Turns out this bitch ass Italian is the one my father remixed for that bread a while back. He doesn't just want the fucking keys. He wants the fifty million cash delivered with it or he's gonna kill her."

"That's a lot of fucking paper, Ghost. Who in the fuck do these people think we are? Bank of America?"

"The money is not an issue. It's the weight."

"We're just gonna have to push it until we get it, fam. I'll try my best to stay on the lookout to make things easier."

"We're only gonna be down here for a second. Once we get all that we need, I'm going to get my bitch and get the fuck out of the United States."

"Say less, my brother. I'm gonna take a little trip up top and see if I can find out exactly who this Pauly motherfucker is. It's no reason for us to waste time in the same place. I'll tell you everything I find out on the way. If I can find out where she is before you can make it up there, I'll kill whoever I have to and walk out that door with her, folk."

"That's Love, fam. Get at me as soon as you find anything out."

"Will do, folk," Shadow said before he ended the call.

Grabbing his gun, he put it at his waist and headed out of his hotel room. Getting to his car, he sparked up the half smoked Kush blunt and slightly turned the music up. *Ambitionz as a Ridah* from Meek Mill started pouring through the speakers as he put the car in drive and pulled off. As he left out the hotel's driveway, he decided to hit up Gunz and let him know what the mission for today was. Pulling over inside the BP gas station, he parked his car and dialed his friend's number.

Ring! Ring! Ring!

"Whoaa?" Gunz said in a sleepish tone as he answered the phone.

"What's mobbing? Ya'll niggas ready to get some paper or what, nigga," Ghost asked, throwing the roach to the blunt outside of the window.

"Ha-Ha, nigga! What type of crazy ass question is that? I'm always ready to mobb on some shit. Corey is just my name, nigga. Gunz is the Don inside of me."

"Facts. Have you gotten a chance to hear from Mark at all?"

"Nah! Bro split up from me yesterday after you dropped us off. I tried to hit his phone earlier, but I ain't get a answer."

"Okay, okay, listen. I got the movement for today. I'ma need ya'll to meet me at the S and S Cafeteria on Campbellton. It sits right at the top of the plaza. When y'all get there, I'll discuss what's good after we eat a meal or some shit. I'll be there in like an hour and a half, so make sure Mark's slow ass is on point."

"I got you, bro. You know I'll find him. I just gotta get up and get dressed real quick."

"Cool. Aye, look, don't forget a look means everything. So, make sure you and Mark's country ass are looking presentable and not like we finna lay some shit down."

"I got you, bro. That's already done," Gunz said, ending the call.

Chris Green

Chapter 7

Pulling up on Cleveland Avenue, Dev made a left turn by the CVS and parked in front of the third house on the street.

"Where in the fuck are we?" Pooch asked, looking around at the houses.

Dev laughed hard, knowing Pooch wasn't used to this type of environment. Being stuck around so many tall buildings and packed traffic would program you that way. "This is Cleveland Avenue. I heard it supposed to be a high rate for bloods around this area. So, we gotta stay low key for real."

"If you know this a blood strip, why in the fuck are we over here, Dev?"

"Because, son, we need a duck off spot. We don't know anyone down here. This is the only family member I have in Atlanta and he's gonna be the one who help us navigate our way through these streets."

David made his way outside on the porch as Dev and Pooch stepped out of the car. "Cuzzo! What the fuck going on?" he said with a smile as he grabbed Dev in a hug.

"What's good, family. How you been?"

"Man, just maintaining. You know shit ain't been the same since JC passed away. I been trying to make it through. Who this you got with ya'?"

"Pooch, this is my cousin David. Pooch is my young nigga from the Bronx. He's like my little brother."

"What's good, bro?" David said, giving the young kid a firm handshake.

"Nun much, my guy. I was hoping you could show me around this city a little bit. Never been down this way before, but it's always good to try new things. Ya' dig?"

"Most def! Y'all niggas good, man. My home is y'all home. Come get settled in and we can hit the Blue Flame or something tonight."

"Good, 'cause I'm tired as fuck right now. I need to crash and get a little rest."

"First room to the right, 'lil bro. Everything you need is in there. Make ya' self at home."

"Check."

As Pooch made his way inside the crib, Dev fired up a cigarette and looked in David's eyes. "I really need ya' help while we're down here. I need some quick paper, if you know what I mean."

"I hear you, cuz. I got a couple people I can hook you up with who got some good prices on some shit."

"Nah, David. I'm not trying to mix in with anyone. I need you to put me on a few cats who sweet, and let me put a little butta love on these pussies."

David couldn't help but laugh, knowing his cousin's intentions. "I got you, bro. Let's kick shit tonight and I'll let you know what I know."

Dev flashed him a greedy smile and put his arm around his neck as they headed inside of the crib.

New York

Pauly moved swiftly behind his bodyguard as they both headed upstairs. Sticking the key inside the hole, the man unlocked the room, allowing Pauly to step inside. He grabbed a chair from the corner of the wall and placed it in the center of the room, directly in front of Erica. Pauly eased down in the chair and re-lit his half-burned cigar as she stared at him with murder burning through her eyes.

"How are you?" Pauly asked, letting out a cloud full of smoke. "You know it was really never my intention to mix you up in this messy situation that your so-called friend has put you in. Quite frankly, if you were my friend, I would be willing to come and sacrifice myself for the love that I share with you, but unfortunately, I'm not your friend."

Erica continued to sit in silence as he ranted on. Her hair was frizzy and her left eye was severely swollen from the beatings she received from her caretaker.

"How did her eye get swollen?" Pauly asked as he looked up at his henchman.

"I'm not sure, sir."

He stared at the man, quietly hitting his cigar, and turned his attention back to Erica. "You'll have to forgive me. I'm not always around to keep an eye on you to make sure you're okay. I'm just gonna get straight to the point. Tell me where your little boyfriend is hiding my money and drugs and I'll kindly let you go on about your business."

Pauly sat back in his chair, waiting for an answer as she burned a hold through his face. She clawed her fingers at the hardwood floor, but still didn't say a word.

"Ya' know something, darling? I don't think you truly know how severe this little confusion has been for me, and if you took the time to really get to know me, you would know I really despise confusion. I decapitate people like you and your family in meat houses, and let pigs dispose of your bodies. You got one more chance to save your people. It's a possibility that none of them will be here tomorrow."

"You won't have too long before he comes up here. You're gonna wish you never touched me," Erica mumbled through her dry lips.

Pauly began to laugh evilly as he rubbed his hand through the top of his head. "You sound so sure about this little companion of yours. I'm gonna fill you in on a small secret. Things that you do in life will always effect the people who are close around you. The decisions you decide on, could be your last. I'm starting to feel that you people just don't care about the respect I deserve. I think you'll understand a little better when your family's bodies start falling down upon your head. I run a very lucrative business. When things start falling from this empire, it makes me look like a failure. I want you to know that I gave you a choice to make. You chose to be a bull-headed bitch which kinda makes you look stupid. Are you sure you wanna play this game with me?"

The words that he spoke made Erica's stomach bubble in fear. It had already been four days since she was taken from the family and still hadn't heard a word about Ghost coming to get her. Reality started to kick in and she began to wonder if the love of her life was still on her side. Finding out that she was a Federal Agent ripped Ghost's spirit and heart away from her. Every day she knew. The distance was getting further apart. She held her head down and started to accept the fact that she might die right in the room she sat in.

"I take your quietness as your answer. Obviously, nothing that is happening around you matters. If my money and my product isn't delivered to me within the next month, I'm gonna chop up your body and feed you to the customers inside of Patsy's. If you really knew who I am, then you would have some understanding and show me some fucking respect," Pauly said in his Italian accent.

Standing out of his chair, he fixed his collar and adjusted the sleeves on his shirt. After whispering in his henchmen's ear, he opened the door and left the room. The guard stood in the corner with his arms folded as he continued to stare at Erica. This sick urge in his head began to build as he stared at her curvy body through her clothes. Beads of sweat began to form on his head as he rubbed his hands back and forth. Pulling the keys out of his pocket, he moved swiftly over towards her and began to unlatch the locks around her feet. Erica slid back in fear as he began to snatch at her pants to pull them down.

"Get the fuck off me!" Erica screamed as she moved her feet back and forth from the grasp of his hands.

Using her left foot, she kicked the guard in the middle of the forehead, making him stumble back just a little.

"You stupid fucking bitch!" he roared, crashing a closed fist down on her other eye.

Grabbing her by the hair, he spat in her face and slammed a hard-open hand across her cheek, knocking her into a dizzy slur. He wasted no time snatching off her pants and throwing them in the corner of the room. Crawling on the floor with her, he unzipped his pants and forced himself inside of Erica's womanhood.

"Aghhhh!" she howled out in pain as he began to thrust inside of her forcefully.

Tears began to spill from her eyes as she shook uncontrollably from his grasp. His nails began to dig in the side of her hips as he pumped forcefully and released himself inside of her.

Catching his breath, he stood up and fixed his pants as he looked down into her eyes "I'll be back to see you and bring your food up. Please keep your mouth closed. I don't wanna see you die in this place," he said coldly before he walked out of the room.

Pulling her legs closer to her body, she fidgeted from the pain of the deep scratches. "Chanceee!" she yelled to the top of her lungs as she burst into a river of tears. The only thing she wanted was to see Ghost slide through the door and end the situation that was at hand, but the gut feeling she had inside of her stomach said that it was too late for them all.

S and S Café
Campbellton Road Plaza

Ghost had just finished his cigarette in the smoking section of the restaurant after he explained the details of the move they were about to pull. Gunz made sure he kept an eye out for any false movements as he listened to the instructions carefully.

"It's only gonna be six barbers in the shop. We ain't trying to kill no civilians. Give or take, I know they got about eighty thousand in the safe that sits in the back."

"This is a barbershop we talking about, right?" Mark asked, looking kind of confused.

"Yes, but I've been around these niggas for years. I got a person who works on the inside and he said a couple of these niggas be toting some fire. If we move in quick, we can get that shit and be out of there in a few minutes."

"How da fuck do we supposed to know who got burners or not? We moving in kind of blind on this. Somebody gone get shot regardless," Gunz said, keeping it real.

"I don't give a fuck about anyone getting shot, but that doesn't mean shoot, my nigga. All I want to do is get in there and back out. We don't have time to be catching unnecessary bodies if it's not called for."

"So what time we taking off, 'cause it ain't no point of just sitting here," Mark replied, ready for whatever it took to get the paper.

"It's just a little too early. We gone head out around six o'clock. I need less people in the way as possible. I'm not tryna run in there when it's forty fucking people in there, crowded with kids and shit. It'll be too easy to identify us."

After the men came to an understanding about their mission, Ghost paid the check for their meals and left.

Walking back outside the car, he took one last look at the barbershop before he got in and pulled off.

***

Tiffany sat in the master bedroom of the house and searched her phone book for the number she was looking for. After locating them, she dialed the number on her cell and waited for someone to pick up.

"Hello?" the male answered calmly in a deep voice.

Tiffany's heartbeat began to race, hearing his voice. He still sounded the same, and from the way he picked up, she could tell he was still the meanest person she'd ever met in her life. She took a deep breath and closed her eyes before she called out his name. "Jimmie?"

"Tiffany?" he replied, quickly recognizing her voice.

"Yes."

"Tiffany, are you okay? Where are you? Tell me where you are so I can come get you."

She could hear the worry in his voice and knew he was concerned. "I'm okay, Jimmie, but I think I might need your help."

"Please tell me where you are, sis. I'll come wherever I have to. It's like I don't even know you anymore."

His words only made her heart hurt more as she thought about the years they went without seeing each other. She knew that she couldn't just up and tell him that she was killing people for a living, but she also knew he would want answers. "I'm down in Atlanta."

"Atlanta? What the hell are you doing way down there?"

"It's hard to explain over the phone, Jimmie. I'm with my child's father and we're kind of in a bind and need some connections on some things."

"Child's father? Are you telling me you have a child now, Tiffany?"

"Yes."

"I'll be there in seven days," he said, hanging up the line in her ear.

Tiffany knew that a lot of things were about to come out that she didn't want to, but the position that her family was being put in made her push all of that to the side. She knew that they needed help with getting Erica back. She also knew that her brother was ready to kill in the blink of an eye about her. The only thing she could pray on is Ghost snapping about meeting him. Both of their tempers were beyond insane. In the end, there was no other choice.

Chris Green

Chapter 8

Pulling up to the house, Ghost jumped out of his Challenger and headed for the front door. He ensured Mark and Gunz that he would be ready before six, and if everything went according to plan, they would be leaving happier than they came in. Walking through the front door, his father laid asleep on the couch with his hoodie pulled over his head.

"Are you okay, son?" he asked, making Ghost stop in his tracks and turn around.

"How did you know this was me?"

"'Cause I can feel your bad energy anytime you come around. Why haven't you pulled us all over so we can address this situation, Chance? We're all still family."

"Because, Pop, this is my situation. All this shit is happening because I took Jesus out. I coulda just left and never looked back, but I couldn't. I hate the way I am, but I love what I do. I don't need no one else getting their name or face hot. After I get the rest of these birds, I'm going to get her."

"Just because you feel you're good at what you do, doesn't mean you don't need any help, Chance. You can't stop everyone. This isn't a make-believe movie. Everyone is not just about to die and lay down because of who you are, son. We have to sit back and think before you make a mistake that can't be changed. You only have a few selected moves in chess."

Ghost looked his father in the eyes as he soaked every word in. His heart was telling him to listen but his mind continued to make him rebellious. "No disrespect, Pop, but a chess piece ain't got nothing to do with me taking a life. I think you've been away too long and need to readjust.

Whoever had anything to do with my child's mother being taken is already accounted for. I don't think I need any help pulling a trigger," Ghost said to his father before he walked off.

Michael knew that his son was cold, but he could feel that demon that lurked inside of him. The same demon that he carried in himself for so many years.

As Ghost walked into the room, Tiffany tensed up as he looked her in the eyes. Her mouth was open to speak, but the words weren't able to leave her lips. He walked over to the bed and kissed all his sleeping kids one by one. Grabbing some clean clothes, he walked past Tiffany as he headed to the bathroom.

The silence that he was giving began to make her blood boil through the roof as she mugged him quietly. Before he could shut the door, Tiffany made her way inside and closed the door, putting her back against the wall. Ghost stared down at her with a blank face as she stood with her arms folded, returning the same glare.

"I don't care about your attitude. Erica is no better. We supposed to be in this together, but it seems everybody got a lie or two they trying to cuff away."

Tiffany's expression began to drift away to sadness as she dropped a single tear from her left eye. "I'm sorry, Bae. I didn't want you to think I was against you. You've been through a lot. It's only so much you can put on your shoulders and bare at one time, Chance."

"It's going to be okay. I'm gonna get her back. I'm gonna fix this family and I'm walking away. I don't want anyone else getting hurt over me. I'm sorry things aren't going the way we planned, ma. I know sometimes I'm an asshole for no reason, but it's hard, Tiff. You deserve a lot and so does Erica. I made a problem that blew past my control. I didn't ever want you to think I couldn't keep my own family together. You all mean the world to me, but my ways have caused so much pain that it's hard to let my guard down. It's stressing to wonder if someone will hurt you all. It makes me crazy at times and I let anger out from all the pressure."

Tiffany wrapped her arms around his neck softly. "Chance, I know sometimes things will get out of your control. You're only human. You can't stop every bad person creeping around the way. You spend your entire time fighting for a purpose that is no longer worth it. We need to move the right way to get her back and leave for good. I need you and so do these children."

Grabbing her by the neck, he pulled her in for a slow and sweet kiss. Their tongues danced inside each other's mouths slowly as he gripped her back. The fire that sat between her legs was about to ignite more as she thought about the love she needed so badly. Getting down on her knees, she began to unbuckle his pants, releasing his dick directly in front of her face. She began to massage his shaft firmly as she put the head of his member inside her mouth. Ghost bit his lip slightly as she began to deep throat him greedily. She looked him in the eyes as her saliva began to drench his rod. He grabbed the back of her head, guiding her down deeper to feel more of her tongue. She took quick licks on the side and back up the middle, placing him back in her warm mouth.

"Mmmmm!" She moaned, getting aroused from the sight of his manhood. She began to speed up, bobbing her head quickly as she held his stiffness firmly in her hand.

"Take your clothes off," he said in an urge to feel her insides.

His dick stood at attention as Tiffany shed her pants and shirt from her body. Walking over to the king size tub, she pulled her lace panties down and hiked her ass in the air.

Ghost followed by rubbing across her soft ass firmly. He placed his hands on her waist as he guided himself inside her warm pussy.

"Shitttt!" She moaned, feeling him pull out to the tip and slide deeply back inside her.

He watched as his rod filled her body with ease, making her ass rock back and forth. She began to match his strokes as her wetness poured down the inside of her thigh.

"Oh my God, Daddy," she whispered as her eyes began to roll to the back of her head.

Ghost long-stroked her hard as her ass quaked against the bottom of his stomach. The pressure in her body finally released as she spilled a long and hard climax on his love stick. He began to slow down as he admired her perfect backside. Her pussy glistened between her ass cheeks as he pulled out of her, standing up.

Grabbing her hand, he walked slowly to the shower as he kissed her lips gently over and over. He twisted the knob, making the crystal warm water shoot out of the shower head. Stepping in, Ghost pulled Tiffany by the waist towards him as the steamy water ran across his back. Placing her arms around his neck, he lifted her gently off the shower floor and entered back inside her warm juice box. The feeling from Ghost's manhood took her into a euphoric state of mind as he touched the bottom of her stomach. She locked her arms around his neck tighter, putting her nails in his skin.

"I'll kill you before you leave me," Tiffany moaned, looking him deeply in the eyes.

He continued to bounce her in the air, sliding inside her forcefully as he sucked on her neck. Putting her down, he sat on the small shower stool and placed her on top of him. Tiffany began to grind quickly on him as he rubbed her nipples firmly with his thumb and index finger. Throwing her head back in satisfaction, she began to bounce, feeling his monster climb inside of her. Feeling his nut about to come, he grabbed one of her shoulders and one ass cheek as he began to pound in her forcefully releasing himself. Tiffany panted hard as she leaned on his chest, trying to catch her breath.

"I have to finish this," he said calmly, looking at her beautiful face. "I can't stop until we get her back. It wouldn't be right."

Tiffany closed her eyes, listening to the truth spill out of his words. Even though she wanted Ghost to herself, she was used to Erica being around. It just didn't feel right anymore.

"I called my brother to come help us. He was the last option we had on this connection for the supply," she mumbled, trying to see how he felt about the situation.

"Why would you try and bring more people into something we are already losing? You're only putting more people's lives in danger, Tiffany."

"He isn't gonna stop until he knows I'm okay. I know you could use him, Ghost. My brother isn't the average street thug. He's gonna stick with you on the strength of me. Please, Daddy!"

Ghost nodded as he proceeded to bathe in the hot shower water. After they both sat in the water for thirty minutes, they hopped out and started to get dressed.

"I need you to take it easy, Tiffany. If your brother helps, cool, but I don't want you involved in any of this. Shit is just too risky, boo."

"You're not the only protector of this family, Chance. I'm tired of you shutting me out. We have to be open about this, remember?" Tiffany said, catching a slight attitude.

"I'm not shutting you out of anything and I'm being open with you as much as possible. You're to stay out of this and maintain for our kids. If me, you and Erica are all dead, who will they have, ma? Think with your head, not your heart." Standing up from the bed, Ghost grabbed his gun, placing it on the side of his hip. "I love you, but I know what's best, ma. Trust me. After I'm finished with this, everything is gonna go back to normal."

Tiffany sat back on the bed as Ghost left out of the room as quickly as he came. Her mind was telling her to listen to what her companion wanted her to do, but the heart was screaming for her to kill everyone until they brought Erica back home. Grabbing the joint off the dresser, she put it to her lips and sparked the Kush.

Walking out the house, Michael stood on the front porch with his arms folded across his chest. "Do you need me to come with you?" he questioned, looking at Ghost seriously.

"Not right now, Dad. I promise I'm not shutting you out. I just don't want to spill you into this messy shit and you fall because of me."

"I was mixed into it the day I became your father, Chance. The same way you want to protect your family, I want to protect my children. I'm here if you need me."

The sound of Suave's Mustang quaked through the air as he pulled into the parking lot.

"I got you, Pop. I promise," Ghost replied as he watched Suave get out of the car and walk towards them.

"Whoa, what's mobbing, Don?" Suave asked, giving Ghost a brotherly hug.

"Us. I'm almost there with getting this weight up to head up top. I just need y'all to fall back into the background until the real situation presents itself."

"Whatever you need us to do, consider it done, bro. I got a jugg for tonight on some pies and I know it'll help right about now."

"Handle that and stay close around. We have to keep our eyes open for everything."

"Will do, my nigga."

Michael and Suave watched as Ghost climbed inside his Challenger and skated off.

"I need your help," Michael said, looking over at Suave.

"You don't have to do nothing but lead and I'll follow."

"You mind if I drive?"

Suave dug in his pockets, pulling out his car keys, tossing them in the air. "Where we going?"

"To Home Depot."

"What the fuck we about to do? Build a house or something?"

"Nah, we about to dig one up."

Brooklyn, New York
5 10 p.m.

Lockz sat in the living room of his apartment as New Jack City played on the projector screen. Taking a sip of his 1800 Tequila he thought about the way that he would boss shit around like Nino Brown after this mission was done. Putting in major work wasn't easy, but from the promises that Pauly made to him, everything was already picture perfect.

Feeling his phone vibrate, he eased his hand inside his front pocket, grabbing it quickly. "What's crackin'?"

"Nun much. A whole bunch of crippin'. What it C like?" Dev asked quietly through the phone.

"I'm just sitting back, waiting. Is everything breezy through that way?"

"We good. We at one of my people's spot, laying low. Cuz gone guide us around this bitch so we can get a little familiar on this playground."

"Well, listen. Stick to what we talked about. Any extra shit gonna cause to much attention. That's not our home. So, treat it like our enemy. All y'all gotta do is follow this nigga and peep his movements. Stay out of sight so this shit can be done and over with. I wanna see y'all niggas make it back to the Bronx."

"Listen, homie. As long as I'm with Pooch, we gonna get back to the spot safe and sound. Just keep giving me the info I need and let me handle the rest."

"That's my nigga. As soon as I find out everything, you'll know."

"Understood," Dev said, hanging up the line.

Sitting his phone down on the couch, he took the last swallow of his drink and took a deep breath. He felt bad for sending Dev and Pooch on a mission he was supposed to handle personally. What Pauly didn't know wouldn't hurt. All they had to do was stay on the objective and he would be five million dollars richer.

***

As the woman stepped on the private jet, she took the phone from her bodyguard's hand and placed it up to her ear. "Is it handled yet?"

"No, ma'am. Both of the men are dead."

"They ambushed them at a gas station parking lot and they still couldn't kill these motherfuckers?"

"I'm hiring some more men today. Everything's gonna be okay, Eva. Just give me a minute to contact a few people."

"Mmm, sounds good. I'm on my way down there now. So, if they aren't dead by the time I arrive, I'm gonna slit your fucking throat and watch you drain out, you fucking prick. Comprende?" she yelled in her Spanish accent.

"Yes, ma'am. I understand."

"Good."

Handing the phone back to her guard, she took a swig of her soft Moscato Champagne as she thought about how Ghost and D-Lo would face a horrible death.

Chris Green

Chapter 9

A-NU-U Barbershop
6:00 p.m.

Pulling into Campbellton's Plaza, Gunz parked the car, backing in to an empty space. Cutting the engine off, he grabbed his gun from the middle console as Ghost put the clip into his pearl handled glock.

"Let's move as quickly as possible. It's too many cops that lurk at the top like this, so we gotta stick and move," Ghost said with authority.

"Can we go now?" Mark asked anxiously.

Ghost took one last look around their surrounding before he nodded. Stepping out the car, they walked calmly through the center lot. Walking in the shop, Mark was the first to set an example by striking a barber in the face. Everybody's movements froze, watching the man hit the floor as Gunz instructed everyone to get on the ground.

"If yo' stupid ass don't wanna die, put your fucking tongue on the floor."

Ghost moved swiftly over to the main barber, watching him look up from the spot he laid in. "Wassup, Biggz! Can I please have this shit so I can go?"

"Ghost, what the fuck are you doing? What's the meaning of this shit?" he asked paranoid, looking around at the men with guns.

Even though Mark stood by the door, he kept his eyes moving and caught his victim. The man's eyes laid directly on Ghost as he eased his pistol off his waistline. Before he could even get an aim, Mark crossed the top counter and landed two shots to the back of his head.

Boc! Boc! His gun roared as everyone panicked from the loud shots.

"Everybody! Shut the fuck up!" Gunz yelled, pointing his weapon at random people.

"I said give me the fucking weight, Biggz!" Ghost yelled, hitting him in the face with the gun. Jacking him up to his feet, he began to walk him towards the back of the shop.

Opening the office door, the stainless steel, medium size vault sat on the floor. Ghost wasted no time shooting him in the foot and kicking him towards the safe.

"Agghhhh!" he yelled, falling head first into the steel, trying to grab his toes. The pain began to thump harder as blood started to flood his shoe.

"Open that shit 'for I pumpkin head yo' stupid ass!"

Biggz instantly reached for the dial and placed in the code, cracking the safe. Pulling the door fully open, Ghost stared at the money and bricks that was stuffed inside. Taking the garbage bag from his pocket, he began to dump everything in as quickly as possible.

"Ghost, we ain't neva had no beef. You know what's coming behind this shit!"

"Yeah, yeah, ya' momma already told me. Shut the fuck up, duck ass nigga." After he cleared the safe, he politely closed it back and looked down at Biggz. "Now, was that shit hard?"

"Fuck you, nigga!"

"I know. Just to let you know, this shit isn't personal. I need you to fall back and keep your life. I've known you for some time, but if you step back in my way I'll do what I have to." Walking from the back, Ghost looked at all the victims on the floor as he headed for the door. Before he walked out, he looked at Gunz and Mark. "We gotta hurry up and get the fuck outta here."

Getting back to the whip, Ghost dropped the bag in the trunk and jumped in the car as Gunz took the driver seat. As they sped out of the plaza, he turned left, heading down Delowe Drive and jumped on the expressway.

Lockwood Drive S W, Atlanta
30 minutes later

The smell from the leaky pipes in the basement lingered in the air as Suave and Michael stepped inside the narrow space under the house.

"What the hell are we doing down here?" Suave asked, looking around at the contaminated walls.

"We digging up fifty million dollars."

Suave smiled from ear to ear when hearing millions. "So this is where you buried the stash? How the fuck would we even know where to start?" he asked, looking at the thick dirt under their feet.

"The two medal rods stuck in the ground on both sides of the basement are six feet deep. I buried the stash about five feet in between this space."

Michael walked to the center of the room, looking down at the ground awkwardly. "It should be right here in this spot," he said calmly, tapping his foot on the dirt.

Grabbing one of the shovels from Suave's hand, he smashed it inside the dirt and began to dig.

"I'm not trying to be digging for nothing. I murder for a living, big homie. Are you sure this shit right here, or are you snapping out on some crazy shit like Ghost?"

Michael shook his head as he looked at him and continued to dig. "Can you just help me and have a little faith?"

"Faith ain't gonna help my ass with digging a five-foot hole."

Suave joined in, mashing his shovel into the ground. The top part of the ground was a little stiff to dig into at first, but once they got through the first layer the rest began to loosen up with ease. The job was moving slow, but after a full hour passed, the discouragement began to kick in.

"No disrespect, bro, but we been shoveling this shit for the past hour and I ain't seen a glimpse of nothing yet."

"It's here. I know it is," Michael said as he continued to work on the hole.

Suave posted up against the wall of concrete and looked at Michael as if he was pathetic. "Listen, you've been gone for over twenty years. How do you know this shit hasn't been torn down and rebuilt two times since?"

"Because the house is still the same way I left it."

Before he could finish speaking, the shovel slammed down on a hard layer, making Michael pause. Throwing the tool out of the hole, he began to get on his knees and pull at the dirt with his hands. "I got it!" Michael said excitedly.

Suave dropped his shovel and made his way over to the hole quickly looking in. Both men smiled in satisfaction after seeing the edge of a silver briefcase.

"Thank God! I thought I was about to turn into Bob the Builder around this motherfucker."

"I told you it was here," Michael boasted, grabbing the handle of the case and pulled as hard as he could. The slippery dirt let loose of the case, making Michael stumble backwards and fall. "Bingo! Now we can get the fuck outta here," Michael said, standing to his feet and jumping out the hole.

"What? How many more of those down there?"

"This is it right here."

"Hold up. Ain't no way in fuck fifty million dollars can fit in that small ass briefcase." Suave scratched his head in confusion as Michael nodded and walked out of the basement.

Blue Flame Strip Club
10:30 p.m.

"Didn't I tell ya' you was gone like this shit, son!" Dev said, looking over at Pooch who was getting a dance from a big booty chick.

"Yo', shorty nice. I wanna take her with me," Pooch replied, rubbing on the chick's ass.

The stripper slowly grinded on him as she flashed a sexy smile.

"What's good, ma? You wanna roll with me tonight?"

"I don't even know you. How I know you ain't no rapist or some shit?"

"Bitch, do I look like I take pussy? I'm a fucking boss, sweetie," he mumbled, pulling of wads of cash.

"I hear ya'."

After looking at his watch, Pooch looked over at Dev. "You ain't heard nothing on this nigga Ghost yet?"

"Nah! Don't even worry about that shit tonight. Just sit back and enjoy yourself. I talked to Lockz and he said he'll get at me when he finds anything out."

Pooch decided to listen to Dev and let his urge for some action rest. He took his attention back to the woman in front of him and began to grip her ass as he whispered in her ear. He could tell her vibe had instantly changed from the way she stood up off him.

"Damn, ma, what the fuck done got into you?" he asked, looking at her funny.

"Uhh, your dance is up! The song went off," she replied, saying the first thing that came to mind.

"But I thought you was about to let me take you out for a good night, shorty?"

"It's not that easy," she giggled, pulling the money from both of her thigh garters.

"Wait, at least let me take you out tomorrow to get something to eat. How about that?"

"Maybe. You must gonna pop back up at the club or somethin'?"

"Just put your number in my phone. If I take you out tomorrow and you enjoy yourself, you gotta give me a chance.

"And what if I don't?"

"Then you can act like I'm dead and never speak to me again."

"Sounds reasonable," she said, taking the iPhone out of his hand and entered her number. Smiling at Pooch, she waved her fingers lightly as she headed off into the midst of the club.

"Now that's some ass that I wouldn't mind having spent the night with me."

Dev chuckled a quick laugh as he paid the dancer for her song. "Trust me, after this shit is done, you can take all the ass you can carry back to the Bronx, kid."

"So, what ya'll niggas think? The A is nice, right?" David said, breaking up their conversation.

"Nigga, this shit is bonkers. I ain't never seen so many bad ass chicks in the city like this," Dev replied, standing up.

"Well welcome to Atlanta, cuzzo. This is the land of all opportunities."

"Well, I'm about ready to dig in a little piece of this land. When does the action start?" Pooch asked, pulling out his Kool cigarettes.

"Don't worry. I got y'all boys some nice plays set up tomorrow for some paper. If y'all want, I can turn you on to my nigga who really getting it in."

"No extra niggas. All we need is me and Pooch."

"Say less. Let's get the fuck outta here so I can spill y'all niggas this drank."

"You ain't gotta tell me twice," Pooch said, jumping up.

As all three of the men made their way out of the club, the stripper moved quickly, rushing to the bathroom. She kept her eye on the entrance for about five extra seconds before she walked in, locking the door behind her. Finding the number in her phone, she trembled nervously, pressing dial.

"Whoa," D-Lo answered.

"Ghost?"

"Nah, hold on. Here, bro," she heard him say in the background.

"Whoa, who dis?"

"Ghost, its Tweety."

"Tweety. What's good, ma? How you like Alabama?"

"I'm not in Alabama, I'm in Atlanta. Ghost, there is something going on," she said softly, hearing someone knock on the restroom door.

"How in the fuck did you get to Atlanta? Where are you? I'm down in the A right now."

"I know."

"What? How did you know I was here?" Ghost asked, trying to see if she was following him.

"Because two dudes who came in the club were talking about you. I tried to listen, but one of the men wouldn't speak on it."

"Who the fuck are they?"

"I don't know, Ghost. They sounded like they were from somewhere else. Like another state or something."

"Tweety, where do they sound like they're from?"

"They sound like they're from New York or Jersey."

The line went quiet as Tweety held the phone, waiting on a reply. "Ghost?"

"I heard you. Meet me at the Waffle House in the morning off Old National. I'll be there at eight o'clock," Ghost said, hanging up.

As Ghost sat his phone back on the table, he looked around at Suave, D-Lo and his father. "They're down here," he said, putting the last two bricks in a bag.

"Who?" D-Lo asked.

"The niggas who work for the Italians."

"How do you know that?" Michael asked quickly.

"Because the bitch from the strip club just told me so. I don't think it's too many New York niggas who down here looking for Ghost. Or am I just trippin'?"

D-Lo knew that the pressure was bound to come. It was plain and clear on what they had to do in his mind. "I'm tired of playing with these niggas, bruh. Fuck the Italians, fuck the niggas in New York and fuck these niggas in the A. Let's just kill these fuck niggas and get it over with."

"We can't just do that. If we do something stupid, they're bound to kill her immediately."

"If that was the case then why hasn't he killed her? He wants the money that's owed to him. He's trying to make an excuse, not an example."

"Fifty million and two hundred keys is enough to make our entire family an example."

"Yeah, but holding someone for ransom isn't. It shows vulnerability. It shows that he doesn't know how to come at us. He's trying to hold Erica and send people at us because he has something we want. But we have something he needs. Dad, show him."

Michael walked around to the head of the table and pulled a soft black pouch out of his pocket. Opening it up, he poured the sparkly crystal diamonds in his hand and laid them down gently.

Ghost's eyes lit up with instant dollar signs as he looked down at the priceless stones. Picking one up, he stared at it closely and looked over at his father. "Where did you get these from and how much are they worth?"

"I went digging for them and they're worth fifty million dollars."

Ghost beamed at him with an amazed look as everyone sat around quietly staring at the jewels. "You stole these from Pauly?"

Michael flashed a small smile and tossed him the small bag. "Your brother is right. Pauly wants these diamonds. But on the same note, he's heartless. I think we need to put a little push on rescuing this girl."

Knowing his father was right, he began to slide all of the gems into the pouch and tied it into a knot. "Let's get the rest of this weight up so I can go and get her back. If anyone steps in our path along the way, then do what's necessary, so they won't step in our way again."

"I got something I'm supposed to be sliding down on right now. It's too sweet and I know it'll do a little justice on what we tryna come up with," Suave said, heading for the door.

"You don't want nobody to mobb with you?"

"Nah, Don, everything Mafioso. This shit easy. It'll be done before tomorrow night. I just gotta do a little homework and its sealed."

"Just keep us posted and pull back up as soon as possible."

Suave nodded as he closed the front door behind him.

"Shadow is already a step ahead of us. He's up there and he's found out shit that might help us find Erica sooner. I told him to find out exactly where he is and sit back until we arrive. So we have our eyes."

"So what am I supposed to do while all this is going on?" Tiffany asked, leaning on the wall.

"I explained this to you already, Tiff. I need you to keep an eye on our kids. It's too much going on to risk you going out there."

"What about Tweety?" D-Lo asked.

"I'm going to meet her in the morning. If anything, I'll make her keep the niggas around just in case we need a hostage or two. Idiots are weak for pussy. If we catch they ass doing bad, they're going to tell us everything about Pauly that we need to know."

"I agree! It's reverse psychology. He has Erica and we have his soldiers and his money. Even trade, no swindle," Tiffany voiced.

"Look, bruh, we with you a hundred percent. Let's just end this shit so we can get sis back home," D-Lo said, trying to brighten the mood.

"I know. I'm just putting together the last few steps so this shit won't backfire on us. I'm going to ask him to release Erica one time, and he can have his shit. If he doesn't, we're gonna split the entire New York City in half. If she's dead, then New York City will be my burial ground."

"She's not dead, bruh, and we are about to get her back. Bad luck seems to follow us around, but we always win in the end. Erica has stuck through a lot of stuff with you. So has Tiffany. If it wasn't for you saying let's move to California, we would have never known our father was alive."

Michael and Tiffany sat back and listened as their eyes drifted to Ghost, waiting for him to respond.

"I'm gonna make sure this family stays protected and solid. Even if it kills me. Just be prepared to get the hell on next week."

Chris Green

Chapter 10

The slight wind that hung in the air the day before was replaced with a thick cutting breeze. Ghost adjusted the collar to his leather jacket and pulled the skull cap down over his ears as he walked into the Waffle House restaurant.

D-Lo sat quietly, parked on the side of the building as his brother walked into the fast food joint. He knew that Ghost said follow him for a reason, instead of going in with him. He decided to stay off the radar and wait.

Spotting Tweety when he walked in, he made his way over to her section and sat down. "What's good, ma?"

"Nothing, Ghost. The same thing as usual."

He looked her up and down one time and noticed that her appearance had changed from the last time he saw her. "So, what was it that you heard last night?"

"Ghost, you know, just like I know. Niggas don't look for you, you look for the nigga. I couldn't hear much because one of the dudes didn't want to keep speaking on you for some reason. They looked suspicious as fuck."

"Do you have a picture or a number?"

"One of them gave me their number. But I'm not trying to call them off my phone."

"Well, we ain't got no choice. I'ma need yo' help with something. You know I'ma take care of you."

"Ghost, the last time I seen you, I almost died. You gave me thirty thousand dollars and I never seen you again until now."

Reaching across the table, he grabbed her hands, locking them inside his fingers. "You know what comes with me. You know that a lot of people despise me. Staying in one spot too long can get me killed. I told you to disappear because I didn't want you in the mix of getting hurt. This shit is on a whole other level now, Tweety," Ghost said with a sincere look.

"Well, how about you let me decide when shit gets too rough for me. Instead of sending me to different states and having no one—"

Before Tweety could get her next word out, the giant window in front of them shattered from the sounds of automatic assault rifles.

Bloc! Bloc! Poc! Poc! Poc! Poc! Poc! The machine guns roared as Ghost snatched Tweety to the floor.

The bullets began to rip down the lights on the ceiling as everyone in the eatery ducked from being shot. Pulling out his Glock, Ghost motioned for Tweety to stay low as he ducked towards the last window. Raising up, he sent a slug through one of the men's chest as he slid behind the side wall from the bullets that began to fly more awkwardly.

D-Lo spotted the action from around the building and wasted no time going under the seat and pulling out the Mac 90 sub machine gun. Jumping out of his whip, he released shot after shot, letting the gun blast rapidly.

Running up to the front door, another hitman with a red mask ran in with his guns blazing. Ghost stuck his arm out from the behind the wall and placed two shots to his back and one inside his head. *Boc! Boc! Boc!*

"Tweety, come on!" Ghost yelled through the screams that filled the air.

The last man that stood by the truck firing his weapon was gunned down as D-Lo let the clip retire his soul.

"Punk ass fuck boy," he mouthed, standing over him. *Boc! Boc! Boc! Boc! Boc! Boc! Boc!*

Running out of the Waffle House, Ghost clutched his gun tightly with Tweety following closely behind him.

"Meet me at the house," he said, jumping inside his Challenger.

D-Lo nodded and started jogging back to his car. Getting in, he brought his engine to life and pulled out directly into traffic after Ghost.

New York
Hampton Inn Hotel

It had only been a day since Shadow touched down in New York and his info radar was pumping off the map. He found out that the restaurant Patsy's belonged to Pauly, along with a few night spots. It was amazing to him what a junkie would spill for an ounce of raw heroin. He only had one mission on his mind and that was to help his friend find Erica. The only thing that had him slightly nervous was that Pauly ran the entire Brooklyn Borough. He even had half of Queens and Harlem. The spooky part about it was crazier. Pauly wasn't even Italian, he was Sicilian. But his power was enforced over both.

Sliding his collar shirt over his tank top, he buttoned it up and slid on his handgun shoulder holster. Looking at the time on the cellphone, he began to flick through the photos of the night spots he was directed to. After sending Ghost a quick message, he grabbed his jacket and headed out the door.

***

Eva sat back in the passenger seat of the Mercedes Benz truck as she answered her phone. "I hope you got good news for me."

"No, ma'am, they failed again. The targets got away, Ms. Ramirez."

Taking a deep breath, she began to massage her temples as she thought about the remedial clowns she had working for her. "Can you please tell me how this happened?"

"It was supposed to be an ambush at the waffle spot."

"And?"

"All of them were killed and let the targets get away."

"Consider yourself dead. I'll handle this problem on my own," Eva replied, hanging up.

"Ma'am, do you want to continue on with plan B?" the driver asked, keeping his eyes on the road.

"Yes, call her and explain what to do. My patience is running thin. I'm ready to end this."

"Right away, ma'am."

***

It was nine thirty when Dev looked at his watch in the living room. He sat patiently as Pooch strapped on his vest and grabbed his two handguns.

"So, you sure this man got this shit in this spot, cuz?" he asked, looking over at David.

"Listen, bro, this man does this shit all around the clock. It may be a few light weights in there with him. Just get him and you gone get the work."

"Well, I hope so. If I push the issue and get in that spot, he gone give up that bread or I'ma spill his stupid ass," Pooch said, tapping on his strap.

"Is that all we need to know about?" Dev asked, trying to stay focused.

"That's it. You got the apartment info. The nigga drive a Lexus truck, all black. If that car ain't parked in the front, he ain't there."

"So what the hell we supposed to do if he ain't there?"

"Wait it out, nigga. This ain't New York. You have patience and lay on a nigga, the lick go extra smooth and sweet. You rush and you'll fuck around and get killed."

"You right, it ain't New York, it's a small city. Let's go, Pooch," Dev said, heading to the door.

Looking at David with a funny expression, they walked out, closing the door behind them.

"Do you think this shit is official, cuz?" Pooch asked as they walked towards the car.

"If he said it is, we gone see. If it ain't right, cousin or not, I'll brush that baby!"

Getting inside, Dev crank up the engine and fixed his mirrors. At the end of the day, his mind was on one mission, and that was Ghost. All he had to do was wait for Lockz's confirmation and his job would be completed so that he could head back home.

***

Suave stood on the side of the abandoned house across the street. His gun was dangling in his right hand as watched the two men come out of the house and get into a car. Seeing that David's car was still parked, he screwed the silencer onto his handgun and headed across the street. Walking up to the driveway, he made his way to the porch and knocked three firm times on the door.

David was coming from the bedroom with his scale as the knock on the door got his attention.

"Man, you niggas finna have to get a fucking key made," he shouted, heading to the door.

As he twisted the lock and turned the knob, Suave's foot caved into the hard oak, making it slam into David's face.

Stepping into the living room, Suave shut the door as he leveled his gun at him.

"What the fuck? Who the fuck are you?" The blood was pouring from his nose as their eyes locked on one another.

"Where the paper and the work at, bruh? Let's make this kinda quick so I can head on out of here."

David looked at his hard, cold demeanor and knew that he wouldn't hesitate to pull the trigger. Suave turned his head, looking at the scale on the table and back at him. Aiming the gun to his hand, he fired two shots, knocking off three of his fingers instantly.

"Arghhh! Ahh fuck!" David hollered, rolling on the carpet as he clutched his hand tightly.

Suave still remained calm as he watched the man have a semi heart attack in front of him. "Hey! Shut the fuck up and tell me where the fucking weight is."

David gritted his teeth from the heat of the hot lead. "It's in the TV", he mumbled, looking at the wide screen that sat in the corner.

Backing up towards the wall, Suave kicked the back board loose, exposing the neatly wrapped bricks of clean. "So, where is the money?"

David swallowed a mouth full of spit and his forehead was sweating heavily as he winced in pain. "It's inside the cereal boxes on the refrigerator."

Pweet, pweet, pweet, pweet. The silencer whistled as he placed four shots into David's chest. Suave stood still for a minute and listened to the silence. After he relaxed, he began to move quickly to the kitchen. Grabbing the boxes, he opened them one by one and dumped the blocks of money onto the table. Wrapping the tablecloth around the cash, he headed back to the television and started to collect the keys.

He took his time to be sure that he didn't touch anything but the drugs. He counted them out as he placed all of it in the middle of the thin cloth. After counting nineteen keys, he placed a knot in the center using two edges, and walked out of the back door as smoothly as he came.

Chris Green

Chapter 11
Regency Park
Ten hours later

It was seven thirty in the evening and the sun had just began to go below its peak. Dev and Pooch was on their third pack of cigarettes and still hadn't seen a glimpse of Blake.

"Man, how fucking long does this nigga expect us to sit right here, son?"

Dev kept his eyes on the moving cars around the area. He was close to saying fuck it, but his intuition told him to contain his patience. "I'm tired of sitting here, too, cuz. But we been out here this long, it ain't no turning back."

"This mother fucker better have ten million in that bitch for all this good ass patience we having! We already seen six different niggas run in and out the trap like a fucking Mickey D's. I say let's go in there and spank these niggas boots and get this paper, so we can be out."

Dev continued to ignore Pooch as he focused in on all the movements.

"Yo, cuz, I know you not iggin' me!"

Dev pointed his finger towards the black Lexus truck that was pulling down into the driveway. Pooch's heart skipped a beat as a lunatic smile spread on his face. Pulling out his pistol, he placed one inside the chamber and watched as the car parked across from them.

"Is you ready to go and get this money or what?"

Dev placed his cigarette butt in the ashtray and nodded slowly. They watched closely as Blake stood out of his car and closed the door behind him. After seeing him get close to the apartment, they moved at the same time, stepping out with their guns drawn.

The Social Butterfly
Brooklyn, New York

As Shadow pulled his rental down on Atlantic Avenue, he parked smoothly across the street where the free parking sign sat on the curb. He stepped out of the car, sliding on his dark Ray Ban shades and lit his half a joint. He looked across the street at the small club and noticed two body-guards who lingered in the front. After taking another toke on the Kush, he threw the roach on the ground and walked across the street. The atmosphere was highly off balance from the foreign area, but his pistols under the side of his arms assured him that he was okay.

"Hey, pal, where the fuck do you think you are going?" the tall guard asked, touching Shadow's shoulder.

Looking down at his hand, he thought about shattering it into pieces but stepped back, looking the man in his eyes. "Is there a problem or something?"

"Yeah, it is. I've never seen you around her before. You sure you at the right place?"

"I'm positive. I just moved around here and my friend told me I should come check it out. Nothing wrong with trying new things, right?" He watched calmly as the two guards stared back and forth at each other. He could tell from their funny vibes they thought he was a cop.

"The admission for this club is a hundred bucks after seven o'clock, it's no debating!" the short Italian guard said.

Shadow dug in his pocket pulling out a knot full of bills and pulled one off the roll, placing it in the man's palm. "You take American US dollars, right?"

The guard mugged him a few more seconds before he stepped out of his way, allowing him entrance into the night spot.

"Fucking prick," he mumbled to the second guard as Shadow made his way inside.

The neon lights that bounced around the room gave the club more of a chill like aura as everyone sat engaged in their own conversations. A few stares began to arise as he moved onto the floor towards the bar area. He spotted certain people whispering as they observed him, but still kept his cool as he took a seat at the counter.

"Is there something I can get for ya'?" the white, bald bartender asked, wiping his hands with a small towel. His bow tie was dangling loosely, and a small stub of a cigar burned between his lips. He blew out a thick cloud of smoke as he looked at Shadow, waiting for an answer.

"I'll take a double shot of Hennessy on the rocks and a shot of tequila. Keep the change."

The man looked at the crispy Ben Franklin and shook his head as he slid it into his vest pocket. "Coming right up, my friend."

Grabbing the glasses, he needed, he whipped Shadow's drinks in a flash and fixed himself a small cup of white whiskey. Sliding the drinks on the counter, Shadow took the shot of tequila and tossed it back. Feeling the slight burn from the liquor, he lit a cigarette and started to glimpse at his surroundings.

"So, what brings you out to the Butterfly tonight?"

"A friend told me about it. So, I decided to come check it out."

"I've been working for this place for over ten years. You be here so long that it gets to the point you're about familiar with everything that goes on. I know a visitor when I see one. Where you from?" The man asked, filling his cup with another shot.

"I'm from Georgia, but New Zealand is my birth place," Shadow said, lying, trying to end the question game.

"Well, welcome to the Big Apple, buddy. This is the land of all opportunities on whatever you can think of. You stick around long enough, I can show you a few gambling spots in the area, if you're into making free money."

Shadow looked at the bartender in the eyes before he spoke. "I'm always up for making money. I just like to make sure my cash is in the right person's hand. I need an investment partner. Have you heard of guy named Pauly?"

The man's vibe began to change after he heard the name run through his ears.

"Where did you hear a name like that?" he asked, bringing his face a little closer as he pulled on the last of his cigar.

"To be honest, it's kinda clear on who runs Brooklyn. I've never gotten a chance to meet him in person. It seems like he doesn't like money at all if you ask me."

"I've never heard of him before. Sorry! If you would excuse me, I have to finish tending to these guest."

Shadow watched as the man grabbed a platter full of champagne glasses and a bottle of Remy Martin. He made his way from around the counter and headed out into the crowd quickly. The tension began to get high as Shadow turned to see a group of Italian men with their eyes scoping in his direction. Standing up from the bar, he took the last swig of his drink and began walking towards the door.

On the way out he spotted the bartender sitting in the dark, in a sectioned off corner, in deep conversation with a man he could barely see.

It was obvious that Pauly was well-respected with fear around the area, no one would speak on him, or even give a clue about what he looked like. Shadow reached into his pocket for another smoke as the wind from the outside met his face. His senses told him to turn around but before he could feel the Beretta M9 come crashing across his head. Dizziness clouded his vision as his body collapsed to the ground. Before he could shake the drowsiness off, another pistol hit him on the side of the temple and knocked him unconscious.

"Pick 'em up, pick 'em up!" Tony yelled to the two stupid idiots Pauly hired.

Placing his fingers inside his mouth, he whistled, signaling the van inside the alleyway. Pulling around the side of the building, the Astro van door slid open quickly as it came to a halt in front of the club.

"Take him somewhere and get rid of 'em," Tony said, looking at the two men.

"And where exactly do you want us to take him, Tony? We don't have anywhere to bury him or nothing," the shorter guard replied.

As they loaded Shadow in the van, Tony made his way to the passenger side window. "Find somewhere for him to sleep; no witnesses. Pauly said this needs to be handled now, and there shouldn't be any fuck ups. Right, Johnny?" Tony voiced, lightly tapping the tall guard on his face.

"Nah, boss, no fuck ups."

"Good, that goes for you too, Saul. Any fuck ups and you'll both be sleeping with the fishes. Call me and report after everything is complete," he said, walking back into the club.

As the van swerved off, leaving the scene of the spot, Johnny looked over at Saul with a confused face.

"What? Why in the fuck are you looking at me like that? What's the matter with you?"

"Saul? How are we supposed to get rid of this guy if we don't have anywhere to put him?"

"We do have somewhere to put 'em, dummy. We gotta just find out where that place is gonna be first. Just get back there with him in case that son a bitch wakes up."

Saul gave Johnny an aggravated look as he made his way to the back of the van. Johnny looked at the two rookies making them slide out of his way as he began to search Shadow's pockets. After taking his guns and valuables, a brilliant thought popped in his head quickly.

"Hey, Saul, how about we just take 'em to the beach? We kill 'em, throw him in the water and keep it moving."

"Yeah, that would be great wise guy. If it wasn't a million freakin' people who partied on the beach at night. It'll be out in the open and somebody will probably squeal before we can even get out of the area."

"Saul, today is Sunday. The beach was closed since Friday. They're reconstructing a new boat dock. Remember?"

"Johnny, you're a fucking genius. That's the way you're supposed to think, dumbass."

The rest of the ride was quiet as they navigated themselves through the New York streets of Brooklyn. Saul watched his rearview mirror carefully to make sure they weren't being followed. After he felt comfortable, he turned down the next street, making his way towards Brighton Beach. Pulling inside the lot, the water was calm and the wind felt as if it was going along with the smooth waves that spread into the ocean.

Saul pulled the van up to the new boat dock and parked on the side of the walkway. The shiny lights from the boardwalk that sat over a hundred feet away was moving swiftly as the people migrated to the new restaurant that was opening that night. He knew they were too far away to be seen. So, he decided to make the mission move as fast as possible

Stepping out of the van, he walked to the door, sliding it open. "Come on, get 'em outta here!"

Johnny moved in a hurry as he pulled Shadow out of the vehicle by the handcuffs he placed on his wrist.

"You two just wait here," Saul said to the other guards as he closed the door in their faces.

Shadow's eyes began to come open as Johnny pulled him towards the edge of the dock. He looked at both men through squinted eyes as he tried to locate where he was. His mind was functioning, but his body just wouldn't move. As they got to the ledge, Johnny let him fall to his knees on the floor.

"Hey, pal, I'm gonna ask you this one time and one time only. Who do you work for?" Saul asked, looking at Shadow who was breathing erratically.

The only thing he was able to hear was his brain thumping hard and mumbling words that Saul spoke in slow motion.

Saul looked at Shadow with an evil expression and smiled. "I guess we got a No Give a Fuck guy right here. Johnny kill 'em."

"You're not gonna try to find out who this guy is first? Maybe he knows something, Saul."

"I don't give a fuck what he knows. I told the fucker to speak and he looked at me like I was a piece of ass wipe paper. Kill 'em now!"

Johnny shrugged as he pulled out his 9-millimeter and placed one shot in Shadows back.

Boc!

The bullet made him fall head first off the deck and crash into the water. His body began to slowly float as Johnny placed the gun back on his hip.

"You have to be the slowest piece of prick I've ever known. How do you know he's gonna die from shooting him in the back? Why didn't you just shoot 'em in the head?"

"I didn't wanna get blood on my clothes, Saul," Johnny said, shrugging in a dumbfounded motion.

"Let's just get the fuck outta here before somebody sees us. The sharks should take care of him before sunrise."

Jumping back in the van, Saul smashed the pedal, making the tires screech off loudly.

"If Pauly comes and asks you anything, tell 'em the mission is complete, capishe?"

"Whatever you say, Saul."

Chapter 12

Dev and Pooch were inside Blake's apartment for over thirty minutes and still hadn't found an ounce of work.

"Look, Pooch, let's just get the fuck on, son. It ain't shit here. We already got the money."

"That shit is in here. I didn't sit outside in front of this nigga spot all day to be looking stupid. Tell me where the fuck the weight at?" Pooch roared, hitting Blake across his face numerous times.

His blood splashed violently as he received the vicious blows back to back. *Whack, whack, whack.*

Dev sat back and watched as Pooch spazzed, out doing the most. Blake had already made it clear that there wasn't any keys stashed in the house. He'd already gave up the eighty grand that was stuffed under the couch. He even went as far as giving up his jewelry that was given to him from his dad.

"Pooch, we need to leave now," he yelled more aggressively.

Pausing in action, Pooch began to bite on his bottom lip as he looked at Dev with a face full of rage. "Yo, cuz, are you turning pussy on me or something? This what comes with the lick. Am I right?"

"I said we got the money, now let's get the fuck outta here."

Pooch smiled with a heated smirk and released four slugs into Blake's face. *Poc! Poc! Poc! Poc!* "Now we can go."

Dev shook his head as they left out of the apartment, leaving Blake for someone to find.

"I don't wanna go back to ya' cousin's house, my nigga. I'd rather get a hotel or something," Pooch said, mad about the dope he couldn't find.

"Aite, cuz."

Getting in the driver's seat, Dev cranked the car up, wishing he could've pulled the move on his own. He knew that after tonight, if it wasn't about going to take money from Ghost, then it wasn't about anything.

***

"Aye, listen, bro, I need you to ride with me some-where. D-Lo and Pop went to rent out a couple hotel rooms for us to switch up the status on where we are. I got a few small things we need to handle before we just take off," Ghost said, looking at Suave.

"Say less, Don, let me grab my coat."

Ghost grabbed his pistol off the coffee table, checking the clip before he slid it on his waist. Looking at his phone he saw an unread message from Shadow that he received earlier. Opening up the attachment, he stared at the picture of the building and was totally lost. He pressed the dial button, calling his phone, but was struck with the voicemail immediately.

"Baby, where you about to go?" Tiffany asked, coming to the front with Laylah fully awake in her arms.

Ghost hung up the phone before he replied. "I gotta go and handle something, but it's gonna be quick. I'ma let Smashiano sit here with you until I get back."

"Why can't I go with you?"

"Because I don't need you to, Tiffany. This shit is al-most over and I know you wanna be by my side, but right now ain't the time. I gotta get this girl back home."

Tiffany's frown showed that she didn't like the remark, but stayed quiet as Suave walked back into the living room.

Sitting his phone down quickly, he gave Tiffany a passionate kiss. "When we get to where we going tonight, I'ma take care of you. I promise."

Her green eyes glowed with anger as she nodded and walked off.

"You ready, Don?" Ghost asked, looking at Suave.

"Like always."

As they headed out the door, Tiffany watched and knew that even though Ghost was difficult, she was still one of the luckiest women in the world to have him. She looked at Mariah sitting in front of the television and Smashiano laying next to Bernard on the couch sleep. Making her way over to him, she shook his shoulder lightly.

"Wassup, Su?" He asked, raising his arms with slob coming down the side of his face.

"Do you mind watching Bernard while I run to the store? Ghost should be back in a little while and I'm gonna take the girls with me."

"Sure, ain't no problem, Su," Smashiano grumbled, high off the cherry Kush. He looked over at Bernard sleeping and moved closer to him, getting back comfortable.

"Thanks," Tiffany said eagerly. The house was starting to cut her circulation off from sitting inside so long. Placing Laylah in her car seat, she grabbed Mariah's hand and headed out the door. After she placed the kids in the car, she jumped in the black Impala and pulled out of the driveway.

The man who stood on the side of the house stepped out of the darkness. He slowly walked pass the small bush as he watched Tiffany's taillights glide down the street. Walking up on the porch, he looked inside of the side glass window to see if he could spot anyone. Pulling the utensils out of his pocket, he bent on one knee, placing the thin medal in the keyhole. He struggled for a second and worked his wrist with perfection. Once he heard the lock unlatch, he traded his picking devices for the silenced Ruger 9-millimeter on his hip and slowly crept inside of the house.

Ghost and Suave cruised sixty miles an hour down the road as he thought about the last thirty-eight keys he needed to get his woman back. Reaching down to grab his phone out of his pocket, he noticed it was gone.

"Whoa, bro, do you see my phone anywhere?" Ghost asked, looking around.

Suave began to roam his eyes and checked certain spots but still came up short. "Nah, I don't see it, Don."

"Fuck, I think I left my shit on the table. I gotta turn around. I can't do shit without it."

Ghost looked in his rearview and busted a U-turn in the middle of the street. The Challenger growled as he mashed the gas, putting some speed behind the wheel as he headed back to the spot.

***

Standing inside Ghost's living room, the man looked down at Smashiano knocked out on the couch. Using the barrel of his gun, he tapped his leg, waking him out of his sleep. As he opened his eyes, he was struck with the handle of the gun on the left side of his head.

"Shittt!" Smashiano yelled, gripping his head.

Snatching him off the couch, the man struck him twice in the stomach with his knee and tossed him against the wall. The scream from Bernard began to sound off from the commotion as the man placed his gun to Smashiano's head.

"Whoa! Hold the fuck up," he panicked, seeing the silencer.

As his eyes turned to look at Bernard, two shots was placed inside of his chest and another slug to the center of his head.

Pwet, pwet, pwet. The Ruger spat quietly, draining his life from his flesh.

The screams from Bernard made him look at the couch as he made his way towards him. He reached down, picking him up as he tried to calm his cries. He slowly walked with him around the house until he found the bathroom. Grabbing the stopper from the sink, he placed it inside the tub and turned the hot water knob on full blast.

Bernard started to quiet down as the man rocked him back and forth in his arms. As the tub filled close to the top, he turned the water off and looked as Bernard began to fall asleep on him. Kissing the top of his head, he tossed him headfirst into the scorching water. He watched as his body squirmed with small bubbles floating to the top. Seeing his body stiffen up, he pulled his phone out, sending a message and walked out of the house, leaving the front door open.

Ten minutes later, Ghost slowed down as he turned the car into the parking lot. As he parked, his heart fell through his chest when he saw the front door wide open. Looking at Suave, they both jumped out of the car, rushing towards the house.

Running inside, he noticed Tiffany's car wasn't parked as he stepped over the threshold. His body froze seeing Smashiano's body sitting against the wall. Walking over to him, he rubbed his face, looking at his brother with a hole in his head.

Suave ran in the back instantly after seeing one of their own laying in his own blood. Looking around, Ghost's lip trembled as he thought about Tiffany. Walking towards the back, the breath in his body slipped as he watched Suave holding Bernard in his hands, crying. His legs turned cold as he began to feel weak. Walking over to Suave, he dropped to his knees grabbing his son.

"No! No! Nooo! Please, not my baby boy!" Ghost cried as snot poured from his nose. His fingers shook as he lightly touched the third degree burns on his son's face.

The tears in Suave's eyes began to fall harder as he looked at Ghost, trying to perform CPR on his son. He watched as his friend cried in desperation, asking for his help over and over. He grabbed his brothers shoulder as he kissed his son repeatedly, telling him to wake up.

Suave helped him off the floor as they began to make their way to the front of the house. Grabbing a baby blanket, he wrapped his son up as the loud cell phone rang. Following the noise, he walked over by his fallen soldier where he spotted his phone glowing on the floor.

Picking the phone up off the ground, he answered with tears still running. "Hello?"

"I guess we can finally speak as men now that you answered my call."

The accent rang through Ghost's ears as he looked at the number on his screen. "Who the fuck is this?"

"Sorry. I haven't had a chance to properly introduce myself. I'm Pauly. I can tell by the sound of your angry tone that you received my message. I always thought that Black people could swim, no matter at what age."

The heart that Ghost had in his chest felt as if it turned to lava when hearing the words that left Pauly's mouth. "If you know like I do, you'll pack your things and leave your home behind. I'm going to find you and split your head apart with a hunting knife after I shoot you in your face thirty-two times."

Suave clutched his pistol tightly in his hand as Ghost put the cell on speaker phone. Ghost slid his pistol off his hip, feeling that someone was watching them at that time. The rage began to build in him as Pauly started to talk.

"You seem like a very mean person. I wouldn't doubt that you can complete your mission on murdering a guy like myself. Everyone hates me. Which makes it so beautiful to be in my position, kid. I'm the guy in the spot and I'm the one who's in charge. Your little girlfriend up here really needs you. It's starting to get very cold in New York. I don't think she would like cement blocks on her feet, sliding to the ocean floor at one in the morning. What do you think?"

Ghost clutched the phone as he walked on the front porch. Taking a deep breath, he chose his words carefully before he spoke. "I understand."

"Good. I'm starting to run extremely thin on patience with you. So now the time limit is two weeks to have the keys and my diamonds delivered to, me or the blood will continue to spill."

The demon that laid calm in Ghost's heart awakened as he opened his eyes. His pupils stared into space as he bit into his bottom lip, making it slightly bleed. "I'm gonna murder every last person down to the kids to get to you. If you kill my child's mother, you might as well put the gun to your chin and pull the trigger. Every living thing around you will die daily until I get her back. I have your diamonds and drugs. The two week wait is unnecessary because I'm on my way up there."

"Well, I guess that we will be waiting on your presence."

"Guaranteed," Ghost said, hanging up as he watched Tiffany's car pull into the driveway.

Suave walked on the porch after Tiffany stepped out of the car, grabbing the kids.

"Hey, baby. Why are you out here in the cold with him like that? You know he could get sick." Ghost remained quiet as she got closer, looking him in the eyes. "Baby, what's wrong?"

Reaching for his daughter Laylah, he grabbed her and placed his son in her hands.

The scream that she let out rung through his ears as she looked at Bernard's body and face. "Chance, what happened to him?" she cried, looking lost.

Mariah made her way over to Suave, pleading for him after seeing her mother break down.

"Where were you? I specifically told you not to leave out of the house," Ghost spat coldly.

"Baby, I only went to the store. I didn't mean for anything like this to happen. I just wanted to get some air, Chance," she wept, holding Bernard close to her.

She knew that Erica would lose her mind after hearing that her only son was murdered. She couldn't even imagine the pain that he felt as he sat quietly in front of her.

"Get him down to the hospital and tell them whatever you have to. Let them know that you found him that way, and get my daughter to my father and brother." Walking over to her car, he strapped his two little girls back in their seats and placed Bernard in Tiff's hand as she got in the driver's seat.

126

"Ghost, I'm sorry, baby!"

He forced a smile on his face as a tear dripped down his left eye. "It's okay, Tiffany, your words won't bring my son back to me."

Before she could reply, Ghost shut the car door and walked off. Looking down at Bernard, her eyes began to well up as she put the vehicle in drive and pulled off.

Suave stood on the side of Ghost as he began to place a call on his phone. The sight of his child continued to flash through his head as Tweety answered the phone.

"Hello?"

"I need you to go ahead and do that. I'm on my way."

"I'm getting on it right now, Ghost."

Sliding his phone back down from his ear, he eased it back inside his pocket, looking at Suave. "Are you ready?"

The only sound Ghost got from him was the bullet sliding in his chamber as he walked to the car. Ghost said a quick prayer for his son as he let his feelings fly. As he hopped in the driver's seat, he prepared to show everyone exactly why he was a nightmare.

Chapter 13

While Pooch and Dev sat in the hotel room, they flipped through the bundles of money they struck from Blake's house. Pooch popped his last Zanny when his Samsung touchscreen vibrated on the glass table. Picking it up, he smiled looking at Tweety's name on the screen. "Yo, was-sup, shorty?"

"What's up with you, mister?" Tweety asked sexily.

"None much. Just getting money and being the boss that I was made to be, ma. You must've changed yo' mind on letting me take you out."

"Mmm, something like that. Depends on what you do-ing right now."

Pooch looked at the time and laughed, knowing he would be in some good stripper pussy tonight. "What you tryna' get into?"

"You can come over to my house, if you want to. But you gotta leave all that king baller shit in the car when you get here."

"Ma, look. Just text me the directions and I'm sliding through. All the extra is just wasted air, shorty."

"Whatever, boy. Don't have me waiting all night. I'm about to send it now."

"Cool."

After hanging up the phone, he smiled and put a wad of cash in his pocket. "Yo, cuz, let me see the keys. I'ma about to slide out real quick."

Dev paused what he was doing and looked up at him. "Where you trying to bounce off to?"

"Goddamn. Father, if you don't mind, I'm gonna go slide in me some pussy. Run me the keys, man."

"Look, Pooch, we don't got time to be running up through this motherfucker playing. We got a mission to focus on. Lockz could be hitting us up at anytime."

"Yo, son, we definitely not about to do this. I'm finna push out here, see this bitch and make my way back to the hotel. Simple."

Dev took a deep breath and shook his head. Grabbing the keys, he tossed them to him and continued to flip through the currency that laid in front of him.

"That shit wasn't even hard," Pooch spat, walking out the room. As he headed down the steps he quickly dialed Tweety's number back.

"Hello?" she answered in her bedroom voice.

"Yo, I seen you text something. Is that shit even a real address?"

"No, crazy. That's what we call my apartments. You ain't never heard of the Nine?"

"Baby, I'm from the Bronx, not Number Land. You gotta speak English to me."

"I stay on Delmar Lane, Ninth Ward. Just hit 285 and get off at the Adamsville exit. I'll guide you the rest of the way."

"One," Pooch replied, hanging up.

Brooklyn, New York
11:35 pm

Brighton beach walkway was lit with many lights and figures as people moved swiftly to their cars. Tonight was the moment for the new restaurant Tatiana's to open up. It was an exquisite eatery and bar-club, and the casual lifestyle it presented only made it cool for the proper to be inside.

Coming out of the doors, Chelsea made her way over to the rail of the boardwalk, looking out at the massive water that danced in the moonlight. The thin breeze blew through her long, black, curly hair as she smiled at the scenery. She knew that nights like this were perfect and captivating for many reasons. Reaching into her bag, she pulled out her camera, snapping a picture of the beautiful scenery. The last few people exited Tatiana's as they closed the door, preparing for closing.

Sliding her Gucci pumps from her feet, she made her way down the side steps and headed towards the water. As she walked across the delicate sand, she took picture after picture of the amazing view. Looking inside of her camera as she prepared to take another one, she paused as she noticed a figure laying on the ground.

Making her way forward, she slowly eased in until she noticed that the figure was a body. Dropping her heels and camera, she began to run quickly until she stood over Shadow laying at the bottom of the beach. Her heart pumped extremely fast when looking at the man that laid in front of her. Bending down beside him, she grabbed his wrist, checking his pulse.

After seeing that he was alive, she jumped on her cellphone, calling 911 as she smoothed the hair out of his face.

"Nine-one-one, what is your emergency?" the operator asked through the line.

"My name is Doctor Chelsea Thompson. I'm reporting a man laying on the beach unconscious. We need an ambulance immediately. He's been shot."

"Ma'am, what beach are you located?"

"Brighton. I need assistance, now," she yelled through the phone, continuing to check Shadow's pulse.

"We're sending someone your way right now, ma'am."

Hanging up her phone, Chelsea looked at the mysterious man in front of her. She wondered who could have done something so foul to a person, leaving them to die with a gunshot to the back. Taking her thin jacket off, she applied it to the section of his wound, praying that the ambulance would make it in time.

Ninth Ward, Atlanta, Ga.
12:15pm

Pooch puffed on his cigarette as he pulled up on Delmar Lane. He looked around at all the groups of men who stood around, eyeing his car. The vibe that was in his head told him that the spot wasn't safe. He grabbed his Glock, putting it inside his waistline as he picked up the phone, dialing Tweety's number.

"Wassup?"

"I'm outside, shorty. Why the fuck is all these niggas in front of your door?"

"Nigga, what, you scared? Bring yo' ass to the door."

Pooch couldn't do nothing but smile at her arrogance. "You can't know who the fuck I am."

"Nah, not really," Tweety said, opening the front door.

Pooch watched the door open and stepped out of his car. Closing the door, he began to make his way through the crowd to the apartment.

"You sure you in the right spot, homie?" a man wearing a Goodfellas shirt stepped up and said.

"Hell yeah, I'm in the right spot. You see the bitch standing in the door, right?" Pooch stopped and said. He continued to walk into Tweety's spot as Ghost sat on top of his Challenger, watching.

"Hey, boy," Tweety said as he stepped inside of the tiny kitchen.

"Waddup, shorty? You got all these little fake ass killers in ya' front, asking questions and what not."

"Them just some mobb niggas. They do that with whoever comes out here. Wassup with some of this?" Tweety asked, grabbing his crotch.

"Goddamn. It's like that, huh?"

"Only if you want it to be."

Pulling him towards the couch, she tied her hair into a ponytail. Easing off his shirt, she removed his pistol off his hip and sat it on the table.

"I'm starting to fall for you already." Pooch smiled as she pulled his pants down, squatting face to face with his dick.

She wasted no time putting him in her mouth, sucking extra slow. Her lips began to pull the life out of him as she deep throated his member. She watched as Ghost and two other men entered the door directly behind them. The amazing sensation she was bringing to Pooch made him lean his head back in satisfaction. As he opened his eyes, he stared right into the vision of Ghost looking down at him. The barrel that lined up with the top of his head made him choke on his own spit.

Tweety stood up from the floor and grabbed the pistol off the table.

"So, I guess this what y'all broke ass niggas do over here. Set niggas up for a little paper."

Ghost replied by sending the first bullet through his penis, blowing it completely off.

Boc!

"Arghhh, fuckkkk!" Pooch screamed as he folded over the small living room floor.

Suave and Midnight stood on the sideline as Ghost walked around the couch, standing over him.

"Your pussy ass boss man had my child murdered. You shoulda found out what you were getting yourself into before you came down here."

Pooch's eyes bulged widely as he tried to catch his breath from his wound. His hands shook terribly as he tried to stop the blood from spilling out of him.

"Lockz will be the reason you never make it back to New York. You can save yourself and tell me what I need to know. Or I can shoot you between the eyes and walk outta here."

"I don't even know you, cuz," Pooch grumbled, looking into the devil's eyes.

"My name is Ghost. Does that ring any bells?"

The pain began to hurt worse, hearing the name slide through his ears. His body began to turn numb as Ghost looked at him awkwardly.

"I'm just gonna go ahead and cut to the chase. Can you tell me where Pauly and Lockz is?"

"I can't do that, fam." Pooch said, shaking his head as he sweated profusely on the floor.

"If you don't, you die just like the rest of 'em. Don't be stupid, little boy."

"Fuck you, nigga. You just gotta kill me."

Ghost sat back and watched as Suave and Midnight unleashed their clips into his body.

Boc! Boc! Boc! Boc! Boc!
Blocka! Blocka! Blocka! Blocka!

Pooch's eyes rolled to the back of his head as he took his last breath.

"Wrap him up and get rid of 'em," Ghost said to Midnight as him and Suave headed for the door.

"Ghost, what the fuck am I supposed to do?" Tweety asked with a tired expression on her face.

134

"I'll have someone pull up on you tomorrow and take care of you. You know what to do."

Walking outside of the door, they got inside of the car and pulled away.

"You think we might need this?" Suave asked, showing Ghost Pooch's phone.

Shaking his head, Ghost grabbed the phone and slid it inside his pocket. As he headed towards the intersection of the expressway, six Tahoe trucks pulled in front of the street and blocked him off quickly. Ghost smashed the brakes. The FBI agents swarmed the car with their guns drawn.

"Freeze! Get the fuck outta the car!"

Ghost looked in his rearview at the three Crown Victorias that spaced them in with their blue lights flashing brightly.

"Fuck!" Ghost yelled, hitting the steering wheel after seeing all the agents. His mind roamed quickly to think of something but was ceased from the nine officers that surrounded the car with their assault rifles aimed and locked.

"Just relax, Don," Suave said, taking a deep breath.

"Get the fuck outta the car," a white agent yelled as they flashed their beams on the vehicle.

Stepping out of the car at the same time, the agents rushed in, slamming them both to the concrete forcefully.

"Shit!" Ghost raged as he was placed in the handcuffs quickly.

Suave laid right across from him, mumbling but Ghost couldn't make out his words. Before he could speak, they were both snatched up and thrown in separate trucks, leaving the scene.

1:00AM

The streets were beginning to fade with cars and her mind roamed in a million places as she pulled in front of the small brown house. Looking behind her, she watched as Mariah and Laylah slept peacefully in their car seats. Stepping out of the car, she wiped the dry tears from her face as she held Bernard tightly in her arms. Knocking on the front door, she waited patiently for an answer as she stepped back a little from the burglar bars. As the locks shifted, an older Black man stuck his head out the crack looking suspicious.

"Tiffany?"

"Mr. Watkins, I need your help."

"Tiffany, it's one in the morning. You look terrible and you have a baby out here in this windy air. What's wrong?" Flipping the blanket off Bernard, Mr. Watkins' eyes began to well up immediately. "Oh my God! I'm gonna call a doctor for you."

"No! I can't call the police."

"Tiffany, you have a dead child in your arms! You have to take him to the hospital." Mr. Watkins looked down at the child.

"I need you to cremate him for me."

"What? Tiffany, I can lose my director's license for something like that. Are you crazy?"

"Mr. Watkins, if I go to the hospital, they're gonna ask questions. This is my godson. I don't wanna just leave him anywhere. You're my only option."

The old man rubbed both of his hands through his head as he took a deep breath.

"You know I stopped doing this years ago, Tiffany. Why are you putting me in this type of predicament?"

136

The wind began to cut a little harder as Tiffany looked back at the car. Turning her attention back to the man, she gave in to what she knew he desired. "I'll give you sixty grand. Are you gonna help me or not?"

Mr. Watkins thought quickly, looking down at the small child. Taking him out of her hands, he stepped back inside his house. "I'll see you tomorrow, Tiffany," he mumbled before closing the door.

Tiffany couldn't help but to drop a tear for Bernard losing his life. She knew Ghost was hurt deeply. In her heart, going to the store was an easy way of slipping, and quick enough for anything to happen. Regardless of how Ghost felt, she did something that would keep Bernard remembered forever. Getting back in her car, she drove off to head for D-Lo and Michael.

Chris Green

Chapter 14

The morning light shined brightly through the glass window as Eva stood on the patio of her hotel suite. The presence of her bodyguard caught her attention as he held the small phone towards her.

"Ma'am this is important. You might want to hear this."

Grabbing the line, she placed it to her ear, listening before she spoke. "Have you found out everything?"

"Yes, ma'am, she still hasn't come out of the coma. The doctor said ninety percent of people who are shot in that spot usually don't. She's lucky to still be alive," the woman said through the phone.

"You make sure they do whatever to make sure she lives. There is no limit to expenses on her health."

"That's not it."

"What is it?" Eva asked, raising her eyebrow.

"The doctors did a full examination on her before they performed surgery."

"And?"

"She's pregnant."

The look that spread on Eva's face made her bodyguard come stand by her side. "I'm on my way!" Hanging up the phone, Eva began to grab her things and head for the door. "Lucas, we're leaving!"

"Where to, ma'am?" he asked, following her out the door.

"Back to California."

"Yes, ma'am."

Atlanta Federal Headquarters

It was approximately 830AM when Ghost sat in the interrogation room of the federal holding area. The white, slim man who questioned him for the last seven hours refused to give. He pulled out files of numerous murders and laid them down in front of him as the hours passed. Ghost continued to remain silent until he was allowed to make a phone call to his lawyer, Arthur Harvey. Leaving out of the room, the agent returned after ten minutes and took his place at the table as he stared at Ghost.

"Are you ready to give this little game you're playing up? Or do we have to force you to understand the seriousness of this situation," the agent stated with a cold stare.

"I don't know what the fuck you're talking about."

Pulling the pictures from the bag, he tossed them on the table and slid them to Ghost. Seeing the picture of the dead agent in the middle of the street made him remember that night, and the sounds from the man when the silenced AK-47 tore through his flesh.

The agent noticed his mood change and took advantage. "I guess you don't remember murdering him either? That was an agent. He was the first one assigned to your case."

Before Ghost could speak another word, his attorney and the assistant officer walked through the door. Harvey stood back as the officer tossed the file on the table.

"The director said that he is to be released immediately."

"What? What the fuck are you talking about? No one gave me any order! This man is a murderer!"

"Well, his little friend across the hall just confessed to the murder of the agent. We only could hold Mr. Grey for questioning."

"And it's nothing else to question. My client needs to be released from here, now," Harvey said, cutting in.

"This is fucking impossible. What about the guns we just confiscated out of his cars? He can't just walk out of here."

"Agent, the man who was arrested with him took every charge that we are trying to pin. It's nothing we can do. If we wait any longer to let him go, a civil lawsuit can be filed against us for unlawful arrest with no evidence."

Ghost sat back quietly as he listened. The only thing that continued to tug at his mind was the words of Suave taking all the charges. He knew that he was a true soldier, straight from the mud. But the feeling in his heart made him wonder why he would take the charges instead of staying quiet.

The agent turned fire red as the officer went and uncuffed Ghost, standing him out of the chair.

"I guess we are done here. Good day, gentleman," Ghost smirked as he walked out with his attorney.

Walking through the lobby, Ghost stopped, staring at Suave inside the holding tank. The nod that Suave gave him said everything he needed to know. His gunman just took the fall to free him up.

Ghost continued to walk out as he whispered in Harvey's ear. "Make sure he gets a good attorney. I want you to fill up his books and phone debit so that he can always reach me. I need you to pull some strings and see if you can work something out for him."

"I can't make any promises, Ghost. They have another murder pending on him and his fingerprints are all over the scene. He's headed to prison, no matter what we pull for him. I can get one of the best on his case right away. But I can't guarantee anything on him walking out of that door."

"I'll pay you whatever I have to. Get it done for me."

"All I can do is try, Ghost. You really need to get the fuck out of the states. Go take the money you've earned and enjoy yourself for a change. I'm not always gonna be able to pull up and put my face on you all the time. Your name is ringing too many bells, and if I keep showing up to your rescue, we're both gonna end up in a prison cell," Harvey replied, beeping the locks to his car door.

"I understand that, and your help is always appreciated. Just try for me," Ghost said with a sincere look on his face.

"I'm gonna do all I can to get him back out, Ghost. Let me take you to go and get your car. And I'll get to work on it as soon as possible."

Ghost nodded as he climbed in the passenger seat and pulled out of the homicide unit lot.

***

Dev sat quietly in the back of the taxi as he dialed Pooch's number numerous times. His anger began to rise higher, knowing that he moved carelessly through the streets. He began to regret ever bringing the young one with him.

As the taxi pulled onto David's street, the line of police cruisers that parked in front of the house made him ease slightly down in the backseat.

"Don't fucking stop, just keep driving," Dev mumbled to the driver.

Dev looked out the window as the detectives and Atlanta Police Department walked back and forth inside the crib. The yellow caution tape sent the radar off in his head that something was wrong. Getting to the end of the of the street, Dev wasted no time dialing Lockz's number.

"What's crackin', cuz? Is y'all niggas maintaining, son?"

"Fuck no, it's too much shit going on. Pooch has disappeared on me and I can't fucking find him. This shit was not a good idea coming down here, cuz."

"Yo, hold up, B. What do you mean you can't find Pooch? You wasn't supposed to let the young nigga out of your sight, Dev."

"You sent me to complete a mission with the dumbest asshole ever. He doesn't fucking listen, my nigga. I'm ready to say fuck this shit and head back up top. We haven't heard shit about this nigga Ghost since we've been down here, Lockz."

"Cuz, calm the fuck down on how you speaking to me, nigga. I told you how much money is on the line with this shit. If we back down now, Pauly will cut us out the mix completely of the whole deal."

"Fuck Pauly, nigga. We the ones out here killing and pushing up about that chedda. Not Pauly, not the Italians and not you. Y'all bum ass niggas got me fucked up if you think I'll keep wasting my energy on this shit, cuz."

"Yo, Dev, I don't know what the fuck has gotten into you. Find Pooch and stick to the fucking plan. In the next two days, this shit gonna be handled."

"Yeah, I hear ya'," Dev replied, hanging up.

It was already understood in his head that everybody was moving on their own greedy mission. It was obvious that something was going on at David's house and it was definitely a guarantee he wasn't going back there anymore. He began to think quickly as he redialed Pooch's number, getting the same results.

"Take me back to the hotel," he ordered the taxi driver as he sat back with a heated expression.

"No problem."

***

Ghost was traveling at fifty miles an hour in his Challenger as he pulled inside the medium sized Sleep and Stay off of Old National Highway. Parking next to D-Lo's car, he grabbed his pistol and got out of the car, walking over to his brother who was posted by the door.

"Are you good, bro?" Ghost asked, looking at D-Lo's scrunched up face.

"Do I look like I'm fucking good? I wanna know when the fuck did we get into the line of this business, Ghost? I lost my fucking nephew over something that has nothing to do with him. I'm ready to go and handle this now," D-Lo said with rage running through his veins.

Ghost couldn't help but to agree with what his brother was saying. The look that he gave him made it clear where he stood on the situation. "We're leaving today. The shit is gonna get handled, bro," Ghost said, trying his best not to think about his son.

Michael walked out of the room just as they had ended their conversation. "I know that there is nothing to make you feel better, son. Whoever has to die or pay for it, I'm ready to make them understand that they made the worst mistake of their life. I feel that my grandson lost his life for a decision that I made. I can't sit back any longer. Pauly has to die immediately before we lose anyone else."

"The Feds are on my ass. It's nothing left in Atlanta for us but an indictment."

"What are they saying about Suave?" D-Lo asked.

"He did the realest shit anyone has ever done for me. Harvey said he's gonna try and see if they can work a deal out for him to get a sweet plea. He saved me, bro. If he

144

wouldn't have done what he did, I would probably be half-way to prison."

D-Lo placed his hands on his head as he began to slowly pace.

"How are we gonna proceed from here now? Enough time has already been wasted since we came to this city." Michael asked, ready to get his hands on Pauly.

"I need to handle this shit with Tiffany, and we're moving ASAP. Who the fuck is that?" Ghost asked, looking over at Jaylen posted on the room door with his gun in hand.

"That's Jaylen. He worked for Blake. They found him in his spot dead yesterday. I found that out pulling up to Regency park. He said the only people that knew about Blake's stash was David and us. I collected the last of the work for this whole month, which leaves David in the mix."

"And where the fuck is David?" Ghost asked.

"He's dead."

Ghost closed his eyes hearing the words leave his brother's lips. Walking towards the room door, he stood face to face with Jaylen as he looked in his eyes. "If I can take you to who did this, would you be willing to ride for the cause, lil' bro?"

"I'm right here, ain't I?" Jaylen replied, heated about his boss man getting caught slipping.

Nodding, Ghost made his way into the room. Seeing the huge man who stood next to Tiffany and the kids, he removed his pistol from his waistline. "Who the fuck is this?"

"Bae, chill, this is my brother Jimmie," Tiffany said with her heart jumping from his reaction.

The cold stare that he gave Ghost let it be known that he wasn't going to fold in any kind of way. "My name's Jimmie. You can just call me Jim. I see somebody finally trapped my sister. I guess it's a pleasure to meet you."

Looking at his hand, Ghost gave him a pound with a nonchalant smirk. "Likewise!"

Feeling the tension, Tiffany jumped in between them, sparking the conversation off between the two. "Jimmie, didn't you need to ask him something about what he needed?"

"Right. My sister tells me you were in need of some work in a hurry. This is just a sample of what I got," he boasted, tossing an ounce into Ghost's hand.

Looking at the bag of cocaine, Ghost laughed, tossing it on the bed. "Looks decent, but a zip ain't about to get me nowhere. I need weight."

"How much?"

"Forty-four kilos. Think you can handle that?"

"It's forty-six in the bottom hold of my trunk. Wanna go pull 'em out now?" Jimmie asked arrogantly, holding up his car keys.

Ghost lowered his eyes with a slight smirk. "How much do I owe you for them?"

"One conversation. Sis? Do you mind if I talk to him alone for a second?"

Tiffany eyed her brother skeptically and looked back and forth between him and Ghost. Seeing his eyes shift towards the door, she placed Laylah in Ghost's arms and walked out of the room.

"I respect the fact that you have your own thing going for ya' self and you're not a pushover. Tiffany means the world to me. I haven't seen her since she was sixteen years old and I sat back years and years only to receive a call every other ten months that she was okay and not to worry. After all this time, when I finally catch her, she sits in front of me with her own family."

"And you say this because?"

"I wanna know why you have her and my niece around this bloodbath you're causing. Don't you think that it's best if you push them away from this? I respect your gangsta, but I feel family is first before anything. I have three kids of my own— twin boys and a one-year old daughter. I know she belongs to you, but she's still my little sister."

"Tiffany and Laylah are my life. Along with my other daughter and son, who was just murdered at an age where he couldn't even walk or speak. She may be your baby sister, but she's not the same Tiffany you remember. Innocence looks like that can fool you easily. Which is why I got a bird's eye view over our life."

"And what about your son's mother? Is that the reason you need the weight?"

"Yes. I'm sitting on ice with this motherfucker I'm dealing with. I'm going to New York to get her back and I'm sending her, Tiffany and the kids out of the states."

The respect level for Ghost rose higher as Jimmie listened to him speak. His emotions showed that he clearly cared for his sister. He was even still pushing to get his baby's mother after their child was just murdered. He knew he stood in the presence of a real killer.

"If you send my sister away, I'll ride with you on this mission. My sister gave me a little insight on what's going on. The way I see it, my sister loves you, so that makes you family too. I'm willing to do whatever we have to for her to get home."

Shaking his head, Ghost shook hands with Jimmie as he opened the door to call everyone inside.

Chris Green

Chapter 14

Making their way inside the room, everyone stood around before Ghost spoke.

"I know it took us awhile to get to this point. We've been through things that's knocked our fam inside a hole. I want to make sure after we get Erica back that we never have to endure anything like this ever again."

The ringing of Pooch's phone stopped him in mid-sentence as he sent the call to voicemail again.

"We're leaving today. After all this is handled, I'm cutting everyone their check to do as you please. If you want to take your cash and divide away from us, then I wish you the best. Does anyone have any input on what I'm saying? Or is it clear for us to make a move and do what we do best?"

The fellas stood on the wall silently as they all looked around amongst each other, waiting for an objection. Feeling that his words were understood, he grabbed Tiffany's hand, pulling her towards the bathroom.

"Are you okay?" he asked, looking down into her green eyes.

"I'm ready to get our family back, Ghost. Shit is starting to get too serious with this guy."

"Listen, I know that our luck hasn't been the best dealing with this shit. I love you and I refuse to keep dragging our family through the mud with this. I need you to take the kids and go ahead and leave," Ghost said, looking at her with a stern expression.

"What? Ghost, you can't be serious. I'm not leaving your side with all that's going on right now. We've already talked about this!"

"Tiff, it's not up for debate anymore. I can't lose both of you. Our kids have suffered enough because of me and it's time to make a decision that will help us instead of breaking us to pieces. The house is complete, you have an account already set up and your plane leaves in two hours. I've already made the arrangements, Tiff."

Tiffany's rage filled her heart as she broke down in tears.

"You think this shit is just easy to do, and I'll just walk away, Chance? You made me this way. You showed me what family is all about. Now you're pushing me off somewhere alone and telling me just to leave."

"Tiffany, I'm pushing you away from being mixed into this shit. Don't you understand that!"

"No! You're pushing me away from our fucking family, Chance! I'm lost without y'all," Tiffany yelled while the fam sat back and watched.

Grabbing her hands, Ghost tried to ease her. She tightened with anger flowing through her veins.

"I'm sorry, ma, but me and your brother decided on this. It's no point of you being around this anymore. You have to trust me. If I wouldn't do this for you, my love wouldn't amount to anything."

Tiffany looked over at Jimmie holding Laylah. His expression only confirmed that he was with Ghost in the situation. Her mind began to overload as she slapped Ghost in the face with her left hand. "You've made this shit turn the way it is now and you shut me out like this? Huh? I've stood by your side as your wife through all this shit and I begged you to leave this alone when you had the opportunity, Chance. Now you're making me walk away from the same family you swore that we would have."

Ghost held the side of his face as Tiffany spilled the truth.

"How do I know if I'll even see you again? What am I supposed to tell our kids?" she mumbled, looking at Laylah and Mariah.

Caressing the side of her face, Ghost kissed her lips softly as she mugged him. "I'm gonna make it back. But I can't risk my family any longer. I need you to get ready to leave. Please! I know that you feel you have to be here through this process but you just can't, baby," Ghost said sadly

Wiping her tears, Tiffany bit her lip from saying what she truly wanted to. "Bring her home. You make sure she gets back to us."

Ghost nodded and hugged her tightly. "I promise I will. I need you to get ready for your flight, Tiff. It's time to get y'all out of here."

The frown on her face made it known that she wasn't feeling the idea. Walking off, she gathered up the kids' things while her brother picked up the babies.

"She has your number, so I'll call as soon as the flight leaves. After that, the ball is in your hands," Jimmie said, walking out of the room.

Tiffany grabbed her last bag as she held the room door. Looking back at Ghost, she shook her head as the words came out. "If you don't come back with her, I'll never forgive you."

Ghost remained quiet as she shut the door behind her. Walking towards the blinds, he stared out of the window while she got in the car and pulled off. "We need to go ahead and load up. I'm trying to be in New York by tomorrow." Ghost pulled out his phone and dialed Shadow's number on speed dial.

It wasn't like Shadow to not pick up his phone. He knew if Ghost called his line then it had to be something important. He ended the call after hearing the voicemail.

"Let's just get the fuck out of here," Ghost said, grabbing the two bags full of cocaine. The fam loaded up and headed out of the room. Things could get harder from that point, but loyalty was thicker than anything. Ghost just prayed everything could end peacefully.

***

Pulling into the Sleep and Stay hotel, Dev paid the taxi man his fees and he made his way out of the car. Looking at his iPhone, he redialed Pooch's number, hoping for an answer.

Ghost, D-Lo, Michael and Jaylen made their way down the steps, just as Pooch's foot touched the curb. Hearing the phone ringing in his pocket, Ghost pulled the phone out, looking at the name that flashed across the screen over thirty times.

"Who in the fuck is this keep blasting this nigga shit up?" Ghost mumbled, picking up.

"Hello?"

Dev looked at the phone, hearing the weird voice and looked at the number as he met them on the sidewalk. "Who in the hell is this?" Dev yelled.

His words echoed through the small breezeway as it rung inside his ears clearly. Dev looked at Ghost and the other three men as he dropped his phone and reached for his gun. Before he could pull it off his hip, Jaylen rained a line of bullets through his chest.

Boc! Boc! Boc! Boc! Boc!

His gun slid across the concrete as he grabbed ahold of his right shoulder. Blood began to run through his shirt as he looked Ghost in his dark eyes.

"I thought you would have got out of town after hearing about your young nigga. Two for one, pussy nigga," Ghost said, aiming his Glock.

Boc!

Dev's body crashed on the pavement as his eyes stared widely at the sky.

"Let's go," D-Lo said, as they all rushed to the car.

Ghost looked down at Dev's body as he jumped into the driver seat of the Challenger. Cranking up, he did sixty on the dash, swerving out of the parking lot. Now that Tiffany was out of the way, it was all game in his head. New York was fresh with blood, and the massacre only sat fourteen hours away.

"Do you think she's still alive?" D-Lo asked, looking frequently through the side view mirror.

"I don't know, bro. If she isn't, I'm gonna bury the whole city until it becomes my graveyard. Text Tiffany's phone and let Jimmie know to take off as soon as she hits the air."

Shaking his head, D-Lo placed the call as Michael and Jaylen sat back in wait for the action that was ahead. Ghost slid into the HOV lane, mashing the pedal a little harder. His mind was racing quickly as he gripped the steering wheel. It was only focused on one thing. Pauly!

Chris Green

Chapter 16

"Tiffany, we have less than forty-five minutes before your flight leaves. Why are we here?" Jimmie asked, pulling on the side of Watkins Funeral Home, by the West End.

"It won't take that long, I'll be right back."

Jumping out of the car, she made her way up the steps and walked inside. When Mr. Watkins spotted her face, he motioned for her to follow him as he stepped inside the small room of the funeral home. Picking up the urn, he placed it in her.

"Thank you, Mr. Watkins. I just want you to know that this means a lot to me. I wouldn't have felt right leaving him in a hospital with no one to oversee him a proper burial."

"Tiffany, I'm telling you this because I've known you on a business level for a while. You have to stop the things that you are doing out there. Certain stuff just isn't the same anymore. You spend so much time running from your truth that when it comes back around, you won't even tell what it looks like. It's time for you to end this chapter in your life and let your destiny come into play. You can't cheat death so many times," Mr. Watkins said with a serious face.

Taking the urn, Tiffany turned around, letting the truth soak inside her head. "I'll have your money wired to you in the next few hours," she mumbled, before walking off.

Hartsfield-Jackson Airport

Jimmie waited patiently at the terminal while Tiffany grabbed her ticket. Walking towards him, she looked in his face as she grabbed Laylah out of his arms. Mariah held the side of her pants leg as she stood quietly.

"This is the best move for you, sis. Don't give me that look."

"Nah, this is some shit y'all plotted because you think I can't handle being around. Y'all could have sent the kids off with one of the workers, Jimmie."

"I'm sorry but it is what it is. I want you to call as soon as you land in the islands."

In her head, she knew that leaving may have been the best thing for the kids. But her heart was stuck in the mix. Ever since she dropped Laylah, her bond was unbreakable with Ghost. She never left his side. "If you don't bring him back to me, I'll kill you myself. Since it is what it is."

Throwing her bags over her shoulder, she grabbed Mariah's hand and headed off to her plane.

Jimmie pulled out his cell, pressing Ghost's number on his dial pad. Pressing the message button, he typed in his words, letting him know his next stop was New York. The itch in his hands for blood was heavy. Nothing else was on his mind but making it back.

One day later
New York, NY

D-Lo pulled the rental car inside the run-down hotel's parking lot. The smell of the pissy hallways reeked through the air, as he and Jimmie stepped out of the car. From the look of the building it was obvious that it was the cheapest place on the strip.

Walking towards the room, Jimmie entered the card inside the slot and walked in. Michael, Ghost and Jaylen sat at the table in a deep discussion when the door opened.

"Did you find out which club that bitch work at?" Ghost asked, standing up.

"Facts. I spotted the bitch with my own eyes. Jimmie seen her too. We actually coulda took the bitch, right then," D-Lo said with an attitude.

"It's all good. We're not wasting anymore time. I'm gonna take Pop with me and scope this Social Butterfly shit out. I still haven't heard from Shadow. I know something is wrong. He wouldn't just abandon the plan like this. He's never done it."

"I'm quite sure that Shadow is good. With or without him, we need to move forward," D-Lo said.

"I ain't gone lie. I'm ready to pop some shit. I didn't come up here to sit in a hotel, fool. Straight up," Jaylen added in.

"Y'all niggas need to just relax. We in these pussy's yard right now. We about to bait they ass in the real city way. Slide back up to the club tonight and get that bitch. After we get her, it's ballgame," Ghost said calmly.

"How do you know he gonna even come for that bitch? He might leave the freak hoe. Then what we gonna do?" D-Lo asked.

"I know he gone come for the bitch, 'cause his Facebook said so. That's all the pussy nigga post is this girl. His relationship status is married. This nigga looney 'bout this slut. He gone show up."

"You think he will lead us to Pauly?"

"It's up to him. Regardless, I'm gonna find out where Pauly is. And whether he tells me or not, he's still gonna die. It's a win-win situation."

Standing out of his chair, Michael followed Ghost as they headed for the car.

"Head out by ten o'clock. When y'all grab that bitch, stick to the plan. Trust me," Ghost said, closing the door behind him.

Ghost slowly rode down Atlantic Avenue as he took in everything he saw. It was early in the morning and he puffed on a cigarette as the cold air lingered through the cracks of the door.

He looked at the club that was obviously closed and wondered why Shadow would send a picture of that certain spot. Looking across the street, his eyes locked on the all black Charger that sat alone in the parking space. He navigated his whip into the small section, pulling up next to the car.

Hopping out, Ghost walked over and looked inside of the tinted window while Michael looked around cautiously. Ghost knew for a fact that it was Shadow's car, but it was only one way to be sure.

Ghost grabbed the handle, pulling the door open with ease. Reaching under the seat, he pulled a black Glock 23 from underneath. Noticing that the car was a push start, he reached in the glove compartment and grabbed the spare key that Shadow was known to leave inside. When using the key, he could press the button to give the engine life. He hopped in the driver's seat and looked over at Michael.

"Follow me."

Michael hopped into the driver's seat as Ghost put the Charger in drive, pulling off. Now that he knew it was something going on with Shadow, it was even more personal. Picking up his cellphone, he called D-Lo, quickly listening to the ring hum in his ear.

"Any luck?" D-Lo asked through the line.

"I found Shadow's car parked across the street. I know something is wrong."

"Do you think he got 'em?" D-Lo asked, referring to Pauly.

"I wouldn't doubt it. Shadow isn't the best with following rules, so I know he bucked. If he's dead, I'm gonna die right here in New York, period."

"What do you want us to do?"

"Get that bitch and find out where that pussy Lockz is hiding out. He's our only way," Ghost said, looking at his father follow right behind him.

"Done."

Ghost hung up as he thought about all the possibilities he had on getting Erica back. He knew that time was running out. Seeing the name that popped up on his phone screen, he picked up instantly.

"Did you make it down here?" Ghost asked, keeping his eyes on the road.

"Yes, I'm coming through the airport now."

"Meet me at the small hotel off Bushwick Avenue, room twenty-eight. There's a keycard under the mat."

"Okay, Ghost," the woman said, hanging up.

***

Erica held her eyes closed tightly as the guard violated her womanhood. The stench of his cologne seeped through her nostrils as he held on to her legs tightly. Her mind was so stuck on death that she chose not to even fight anymore. Being saved wasn't even close to being reality in her eyes.

Feeling himself beginning to reach his climax, he pulled out, releasing his cum onto her shirt. Standing up, he fixed his pants as he looked down at her. "You've gotten boring, sweetheart. You can't just keep laying there. You're starting to stink."

Erica muscled up enough strength to send her spit flying into his face. He froze in action as he slowly wiped the glob of spit from the corner of his eye. Balling up his fist, he lifted his right leg, kicking her square in the face.

The vision of stars flashed heavily as she tried to catch her breath. As he turned, leaving out of the room, Erica's tears began to run as she let out a horrific scream.

"Arghhhhh!" she yelled at the top of her lungs as she jerked uncontrollably. The handcuffs kept her restrained as they began tightening up, biting her wrists. Her chest heaved as she closed her eyes. "Just let me die, please," she mumbled to no one as her energy faded.

Her frizzled hair hung down in her face as the blood dripped profusely from her nose. The thought of Ghost began to run through her head. The care that she was given felt as if she didn't even exist. It was once every night that was praying for him to sweep in and save her. But that feeling just didn't live inside her anymore.

Club Lust Strip Joint
Later that night

It was just starting to get dark through the wide skies as cars moved down 47th Street. The club was blazed as always with amazing dimes lined across the stage. D-Lo moved with the crowd as everyone gathered around the groups of different women. He played along, throwing a few bills, but kept his eyes on Catz behind the bar. 2 Chainz's "Love Dem Stripperz" quaked through the speakers as she served a round of drinks at the counter.

The shift for the second bartender had begun, so she walked through the door and she grabbed her bag and phone from underneath the marble top. A few people walked towards her with friendly hugs and kisses. D-Lo took his cue and headed towards the entrance.

Making her way outside of the doors, she moved past the two bouncers and headed to the car. She never paid attention to D-Lo following swiftly behind her. He wasted no time reaching out for her arm.

"Hey, get yo' hands off me, motherfucker," Catz screamed, jerking away.

Before he could react, the bouncer surfaced between the parked cars, closing the gap between them. "Nigga, is you fucking stupid? Don't fucking move."

D-Lo's pistol came from his waist in a flash, placing two shots to his chest. *Boc! Boc!*

Catz's heart dropped to her knees as the man's body caved over to the ground. Her feet tried to move, but stopped quickly as Jaylen slammed his pistol across her jaw. Her small frame fell directly towards him as he scooped her in his arms. Opening the trunk, he threw her body inside. The, he slammed it forcefully. Jumping in the car, D-Lo skated out of the entrance, heading back to the hotel.

Bed Stuy Brooklyn
9:00 pm

Ghost and Michael sat in front of the tall apartment home as the 2007 Honda pulled in behind him. He adjusted his rearview mirror to keep his eyes directly on the car door. Seeing the frail white man climb out of the small vehicle, Michael and Ghost hopped out, causing him to jump. Before he could move, he was grabbed and thrown against the hood of his car.

"What's good with ya', Ronald?" Ghost asked, holding him by the front of his shirt.

"Jesus fucking Christ, Ghost! What the hell are you doing here?" he asked, looking back and forth between him and his father.

"I been real busy. You know I could never forget about my duck. And you know why I'm here."

"Listen, Ghost, I'm not into that anymore. I haven't seen you in almost a year. Things have changed, and the New York Police Department has been on my ass like a cheetah fucking a gazelle."

Ghost pulled his pistol from his waist, placing it at the bottom of Ronald's chin. "Please don't make me kill you. I've spent a lot of money to make it up here, and I've given you a lot of money. Are we staring to act brand new, now?" Ghost asked, pulling the hammer of the gun back.

"Listen!"

"Shut the fuck up!"

"Okay, okay!"

"You've got five seconds to tighten up or I'ma blow yo' ass a brand-new haircut on top of your head."

Ronald looked at the barrel against his forehead and took a deep breath. "Where is Shadow? Is it any kind of way he can talk to me? He's a tad bit more understanding."

Grabbing the back of his neck, Michael head butted him in the nose to let him know that it was serious.

"Fuckkk! Who the fuck is this guy?" Ronald asked, holding his nose as it began to bleed.

"He's the one who's about to murder you on top of your Honda, if you don't get right," Ghost replied.

"Okay. When it comes back to bite you in the ass, you didn't get it from me." Holding his nose, Ronald headed up the porch steps to his house. Walking inside, he shut the door behind them, cutting on his living room light. "Follow me."

Cutting through the hallway, he stopped in front of a room and pulled out a silver key. Ghost stepped in directly behind him, looking at the arsenal that covered the walls. It looked more like a military base than an average white man's room.

"We got nine millimeters, Rugers, Glocks and a few high-powered Desert Eagles. We have pocket toters, small enough to fit inside your palm, or even inside your boots. This right here is a Beretta M6, fifteen shots, quick automatic release."

Michael looked around, staring at all the exclusive artillery that surrounded him.

"What in the fuck is this?" Ghost asked, touching the all black assault rifle.

"That's a federal case. It's a Heckler and Koch XM8, fifty round mag, high-powered duty. It's going through cars and even bricks."

"I want it. I got pistols. We need shit like this."

"You do realize that none of this stuff is free, right, Ghost?"

"I ain't said it was. Are you offering?"

"Not really."

Pulling the roll of money out of his pocket, Ghost tossed it, hitting Ronald in the forehead. "Well shut the fuck up and bag my shit."

Ronald smiled, looking at the money as he picked it up from the floor. "With this, you can get whatever you need."

In the next ten minutes Ghost had everything he needed, from clips, to weapons, to scopes. He and Michael picked up a bag a piece as they walked towards the living area.

"Have you ever heard the name Pauly?" Ghost asked as he grabbed the knob, opening the front door.

"Who hasn't heard of Pauly? The Sicilian mob boss who runs the whole Brooklyn Borough. This is a puppet city to him, if you ask me. I've never seen his face."

"I'll keep in touch," Ghost said, walking out of the house.

Chapter 17

Pulling back into the parking lot of the small hotel, Ghost parked the car and lit his cigarette.

"What if this woman can't tell us anything, Pop? What the hell are we gonna do then?"

"Trust me. Son, it's gonna work. We have to make a move while she's in our possession. Playing with these people is like losing your breath. You never know when it's gonna come."

After nodding, they got out of the rental and made their way towards the room. Jimmie and Jaylen stood up next to Catz while D-Lo sat in front of her.

"Are you okay?" Ghost asked Sgt. Copeman who sat in the corner by the window.

"I'm fine. You might need to check on them, though."

Ghost walked over to his brother, tapping his shoulder. "What does she know?"

"This bitch is stubborn. Ask her yourself," he said, walking off.

Looking down at Catz, the right side of her jaw was lumped up from the pistol that knocked her out. She looked at Ghost in his eyes before he sat down in front of her.

"Look, bitch, it's only a few ways this is gonna go. I need to know where yo' pussy ass nigga is hiding, if you want to make it out of here wit' yo' head attached to your shoulders."

"I'm not telling you shit. Punk ass city sliding mother-fucker. Y'all touched the wrong bitch. I hope my nigga put the whole clip in yo' pussy ass."

Ghost shook his head in disappointment, standing up. He removed his belt, sliding it around her neck and twisted the sides around his wrist. Her eyes began to turn bloodshot red as he choked her with all his strength. Everyone looked on as her feet tapped hard against the floor. The snot bubbles that came from her nostrils began to grow bigger as she fought to breathe.

"Ghost, take it easy," Michael said, trying to get the info they needed before he killed their only help.

Hearing his father's words, he released her neck, watching her eyes tear up from lack of oxygen. "Now, I think we got off on the wrong foot. I'm gonna ask you a few questions. After you tell me what I need to know, I'll let yo' stanking ass get the fuck on, bitch. Where is Lockz?"

"I don't fucking know. Lockz has tons of fucking spots. I only know about the apartment that we stay in."

"The name would be a little helpful," D-Lo said, still mad.

"Crown Heights Apartments, off of John's Place. He has men all over that place. You'll never make it in," she said, with all seriousness.

"That's not for you to worry about. Do you know where Pauly is holding my baby's mother?"

"He never talked about that. I don't know what him and Pauly talk about. Just because he's fucking me, doesn't mean anything. He doesn't put me in his business, period. What are you not understanding?"

"Fuck it, keep her ass here until we come back. If we get out there and the shit ain't right, I'ma kill the bitch my damn self," D-Lo said, heading out of the room.

Jimmie and Jaylen grabbed their weapons, following suit as Ghost eyed Cat.

"I'm riding with them. Just let us see what's going on first before you do something too early," Michael said, headed for the door.

Sgt. Copeman walked over to Ghost and sat in his lap after his dad left. Lighting his blunt from the ashtray, he stared at the scar on Catz's neck. "How old are you?"

"Twenty-nine," Catz replied, squinting from the weed smoke in her face.

"I hear your name is Catz. You like cats don't you, baby?" Ghost asked, looking at Ashley.

"Yes, Daddy, I like it if you tell me to."

Ghost looked at Catz with a funny smirk. "She likes it if I tell her to. You heard that? You're trying to be a dominant, when you supposed to be submissive. Your mind wouldn't last a day in my world. Your misguidance has you blinded by this nigga. I bet you don't even have fifty thousand to your name and he's the so-called King of New York. See, with a nigga like me you would be laced and play the correct way. Your worries about Ghost being there for you wouldn't even cross your head. You've gotten so accustomed to being played with a few funds and think this nigga about to come get you. Watch this!"

Ashley watched as he pulled out Pooch's phone and dialed a number in the call log. Listening to the ring in the background, he placed the line on speaker as Lockz's voice boomed through the phone.

"Where in the fuck are you niggas? Why isn't neither one of y'all picking up the phone, Pooch?"

"Sorry, fuck boy, Pooch was wasted down in Atlanta. The other fuck man with him is sleeping on the concrete slab in the morgue too. Now tell me if you want your bitch back." Ghost placed the line close to Catz's mouth.

"Lockz, please come get me," Catz screamed with tears about to come out her eyes.

"You gone die, fuck nigga. You must've forgot that we got yo' bitch up here. I can blow this hoe head off, right now," Lockz said.

"Yeah, you could, but yo' bitch is sitting right here in front of me. I almost made her eyes pop out from choking her with my belt a few minutes ago. A life for a life, Lockz. Is this how you wanna play?"

"Nigga, is you stupid? I don't give a fuck about that bitch. You think I'm gonna give up a few mill for a slut freak?" Lockz laughed into the phone.

The words that came from his mouth caved her heart into the pit of her stomach.

"If you kill my bitch, I'll just be fifty million dollars richer and the new fucking plug for New York. I'll spend every day looking for you and put a bigger ticket on yo' head than you can count. You give me my baby momma, I give you the diamonds and keys. Even trade."

"You think I believe you got those diamonds? You snatch up this bitch and call me demanding something. You drop that chedda off where I say and I'll give you the bitch. You in my spot, son," Lockz yelled, hanging up the phone.

Ghost looked at Catz as Ashley stood up off his lap. "This the nigga you love so much? What side you really working, 'cause it looks like you jobless."

Ashley walked over to Catz, releasing the handcuffs off her wrist.

"Come here," Ghost said, with his pupils locked on her eyes.

Catz stood out of the chair as the single tear dropped down her face. Ghost burned a hole through her eyes with his as she stood in front of him.

Crown Heights Apartments

"Yo' son, do you know what number Lockz in, homie?" Jaylen asked, standing in front of the building.

"Yeah, he up on the second floor. You should see some little young'ins outside in the hallway. They can show you," the man said, walking off.

"Good look."

Watching to make sure the coast was clear, Jaylen pulled his hat down over his forehead as he waved to the car across the street.

D-Lo, Jimmie and Michael hopped out of the whip, making their way to the building.

"What number he in?" D-Lo asked, crossing the street first.

"I'm not for sure. Nigga just told me he on the second floor with it. It's a few niggas in the hallway. I'm guessing they work for him."

"Follow me," Michael said, heading towards the doors.

All three of them checked their guns as they made their way into the building. Coming up the first set of steps, the man that stood at the top wasted no time pulling his gun. Michael placed one shot between his eyes, making him crumble to the floor.

Boc!

Making their way up, the bullets began to fly as Jaylen began to shoot at everyone he spotted moving.

Boc! Boc! Boc! Boc! Boc!

Pak! Pak! Pak! Pak!

D-Lo released the Colt M4 assault rifle, knocking down anything that was standing.

Baka! Baka, baka, blocc! The machine let loose, sounding off loudly in the hallway.

Michael proceeded to the apartment the men laid in front of. Pushing the door open, a pistol came from the side wall. Grabbing his wrist, Michael crashed in his elbow, breaking his arm. Kicking the gun, he grabbed the man's head, slamming the gun across his eye.

"Arghhh!" he screamed.

Pushing him to the floor, D-Lo moved in quickly, placing his gun to the top of his head. "Shut the fuck up, nigga. The only thing that better come out yo' mouth is the whereabouts of that nigga Lockz."

"Lockz ain't fucking here! He doesn't even rest here, son. I'm just a worker," he pleaded, closing his eyes in pain.

"Where can we find 'em?" Michael asked sternly.

"I don't know, yo'. The nigga never comes around like that. This his shorty spot."

Jimmie walked through over threshold, placing three shots to the man's chest.

Boc! Boc! Boc!

"Let's get the fuck outta here. These niggas are decoys. They never know anything."

Running down the steps, they dashed to the car and smashed off as the neighbors started to pour out. The NYPD sirens could be heard in the air as they fled the scene.

***

Catz moaned softly as she glided on Ghost's dick. Her eyes rolled to the back of her head when Ashley kissed her passionately. He held her waist, making the arch of her back sink. Her ass bounced gently on his pole as he grabbed the back of her neck.

"What side you working, huh?" Ghost whispered in her ear, making her pussy wetter.

Her facial expression spoke for itself as her mouth hung wide open. His manhood stroked her quickly, touching the bottom of her stomach.

"Fuck!" she squealed, feeling the rush of herself cum. Her lips began to tremble as Ashley tickled her clitoris.

Sliding out of her, he stood up as he released himself on her tongue. Catz grabbed the bottom of his dick and placed him inside of her mouth. Ghost continued to lock eyes as she drained every drop that he had to offer.

Ghost nodded, looking towards Ashley. Taking her hand, she led Catz over to the bed slowly, laying her down. She spread her legs, placing her face directly inside her pussy. Her legs locked, wrapping around Ashley's shoulder as the mind games began.

Looking through his touchscreen, he dialed Shadow's phone number as he glanced at the girls in front of him. The answering machine continued to upset him as he felt the worst for his friend. It was clear to see that Pauly was behind it. And it was damn sure crystal that he had plenty of connections in Brooklyn.

Lockz was trying to cuff a freak that wasn't meant and fell weak. It was easy to use reverse psychology based on her neglect from her so-called lover. The sex was easy to finesse, being that she was a slut by nature. Offering her one million for the whereabouts of her dude would make any bitch feel it was time for a change.

All Ghost could think about was the plan his father instilled in his head. He just hoped that it would work. If Lockz wasn't willing to give up Pauly, they would flush the city until he showed his face.

Chris Green

Chapter 18

12:00 pm

D-Lo and the rest of the fellas pulled back into the parking lot of the hotel quickly, and exited the car. They moved swiftly to the sidewalk and made their way inside the room.

Ghost sat at the table with Ashley and Catz when the boys walked in.

"What the fuck is going on?" D-Lo asked, looking at Catz sitting at the table.

Michael gave a sly smirk as he sat on the bed quietly.

"She's gonna help us. I think she's had a change of heart on the fuck man she called her lover," Ghost said, pushing his fingers through her hair.

Catz sat with a clueless face as Ashley smiled.

"We went there for nothing. The nigga wasn't there. It was only a duck off, and ain't no telling how many more he got that we don't know about," Jaylen said cutting in.

"Ghost, we're moving in a circle. We don't know shit about these niggas. And what type of game is this hoe right here playing? How we know she ain't on no slime shit? This bitch just sent us to a straight set-up," D-Lo ranted.

"I know where he is. She just told me. All we have to do is sit back and wait for the perfect time. He's already dead and he don't even know it," Ghost said with confidence.

***

Pauly sat back listening to Lockz speak through the phone, while he took a swig of his hot tea.

"He kidnapped my girl, sir! He's in New York as we speak. This motherfucker has some nuts. He said he's not coming off the debt until he gets the girl."

"So, let me get this straight. You didn't go down to Atlanta like I asked you. Two people who had no understanding of this situation was placed on a mission by your authority."

"But, Pauly—"

"Buts only mean mistakes. It's clear now to me that you are too stupid to handle a task on this level. You say that he has nuts; I have nuts. You know why? Because I'm a man like him. He's no different. Obviously, your nuts have been clipped, because you let a man who we are at odds with make it through the border of New York. That doesn't make any sense to me. I guess if you were a real professional like myself, you would complete the task instead of sniffing under the hooker's pussy."

Lockz held the phone. His facial expression began to tighten while listening to the insulting words.

"Make him pay the ransom and we will let the woman go. If he continues to get ignorant, go in, take it and kill everyone."

"Yes, sir."

"Remember this: To be a millionaire, every penny counts. You start off small until it grows larger. How hard you strive is how much you're worth. Get the package. Bring it back to me and I'll make you a very rich man."

"I'm on it."

Hanging up, he kicked the glass table that sat in front of him to pieces. Knowing that Dev and Pooch were gone put him in an ugly position. He couldn't think of anyone else that could be trusted on a fifty-million-dollar lick. Pulling the bag of cocaine out his pocket, he snorted a quick line while he plotted in his head.

***

Ghost and Ashley posted in front of the room door. The smoke from his cigarette drifted in the wind and his gun was clutched tightly in his hand.

"Whatever he did, he can't go back to Sicily. He's sitting back enforcing his authority over Blacks and Italians."

"And what makes you sure about that?" Michael asked, leaning on the glass window.

"I have an inside friend from the NYPD. She couldn't tell me much, but according to her, a lot of people want his head. In reality, he's the one hiding. I can hear it in his voice, he's pussy. If he was as connected as he say, we would have been dead. It wouldn't be any negotiating. We're going through with the plan. If we get our hands on him, he's gonna tell us everything we need to know. I'm gonna kill all of them until I get Erica back. They started this approach, I'm ending it. I told them to release her and we will leave the ransom for no future problems. They chose to have it their way," Ghost uttered, tossing the filter of the Newport.

"I agree with you. It's no point of even trying to negotiate anything. The line was crossed when he took the life of my grandson. It's no such thing as talking." Michael added.

"Everyone's tired and I'm tired. We're moving out in the morning. All you have to do is watch for movement."

"I got you," Ashley said.

"All you gotta do is lead the way. I'm right here," Michael stated, looking at Ghost.

"It's weird how all of this shit happened. I hate that it came down to family being hurt. For what it's worth, I'll do it all over again just to have you back with us. I'm glad you're here, Pop."

Michael nodded with a slight smile, walking back into the room.

"Just get a little rest. I'm right next door if you need me," Ashley said, walking off.

Ghost stood in the hallway alone, staring out into the open. His eyes begged for sleep, but his mind was on kill. The pain had started to get worse and it was time to end it for good.

Pink Houses
Brooklyn Projects

It was 7AM when they pulled the car down Loring Avenue. Besides a few thugs who hung in the front, the street was clear and quiet of all movement. Michael and D-Lo pulled in directly behind Ghost's car and jumped into action. Stepping out of the car, Jaylen grabbed Catz as they made their way towards Building 1260. Michael wasted no time taking out the two goons who stood on the side steps.

Pwet! Pwet!

The men dropped silently to the concrete, while Ghost and Jimmie took the lead, walking inside. Moving quickly through the small hallway, they began to creep up the stairwell.

Ghost grabbed Catz's wrist, looking at her. "Remember what I said. All you gotta do is get in."

Catz nodded and quickly took off up the steps.

"Dad, come with me. The rest of y'all keep an eye out."

"We straight go!" D-Lo said, standing at the building's entrance door.

Ghost and Michael raised their weapons as they took off to the third floor.

***

The loud knocking on the door quaked, waking Lockz out of his sleep. Jumping up, he grabbed his pistol, making his way to the door.

Boom! Boom! Boom!

Putting his eye to the peephole, Catz panted harshly with her hands on the door. Snatching the latch off, he pulled her in with wide eyes.

"Yo. Shorty, how the fuck did you get here? Did they hurt you?" Lockz asked, looking at her swollen jaw.

"They let me go after finding out I'm not worth shit to you. I'm just another bitch, huh?"

Lockz stared at Catz and began to laugh. "Shorty, this shit bigger than you. You're a hoe. I played my part, now it's time to cut ties." The small knife that Catz pulled from her pocket made Lockz step back. "What the fuck you think about to do with that?"

Catz gritted her teeth as she charged towards him. "Slime ass nigga!"

The tip of the blade sliced him across the chest, making him stumble back. Raising his gun, he pulled the trigger four times, striking her in the stomach.

Boc! Boc! Boc! Boc!

The crashing of the front door grabbed his attention too late. The bullet that struck his shoulder sent him flying to the wall. Michael kicked the pistol across the room, looking around the apartment.

Lockz looked down Ghost's barrel, seeing flashes as he stood over him.

"Where is my girl?"

"Pauly's not gonna give her up. You might as well quit. All you had to do was pay the ransom. Now you're all gonna die."

"Tell me where he is and I'll leave. Don't stand in my way on this. Please," Ghost said sternly.

"You're wasting your time!"

Ghost reached into his pocket, pulling out his cellphone on the video camera. Pulling the skullcap down over his face, he pressed record and handed the phone to Michael. Grabbing the knife off the floor, Ghost began to slice Lockz's neck from ear to ear. The sound of his blood spilling could be silently heard as Ghost stared into the camera. Standing up, he made his way in front of the phone.

"That was your last warning. Release her and take this blessing of me sparing your life to live another day. There is no more debating."

Michael ended the video and sent the clip to Pauly's number. "It's done."

Ghost nodded. "Let's go."

Catz's hand grabbed his pants leg as he tried to walk by. He looked down in her eyes as she trembled badly.

"Help me," she whispered, tasting the blood in her mouth.

"I told you to pick a side. You chose mine and you lost. Maybe you should have stuck with him," Ghost spat, placing a slug in her head.

Pwet!

Running out of the apartment, they made their way back down to the lobby with the rest of the crew. Walking out of the building, they sprinted quickly towards the car. As they jumped in, they crank up the whips, speeding off towards Eldert Lane.

***

Pauly sat at the large glass table in the living room of his condo. The two associates that stood in front of him were in a deep discussion as Tony made his way through the door. Walking across the soft carpet, he made his way over to the desk.

"Pauly, I think you need to see this."

Taking the phone from Tony's hand, he pressed play on the video that sat on the screen. The sight of Lockz's neck being cut open made him sigh in disappointment.

"That was your last warning. Release her and take this blessing of me sparing your life to live another day. There is no more debating."

Pauly looked over at Tony after the video cut off. "This guy is more special than I thought. You give people a way out and they always choose the opposite. I told you when this all first started off that you played an important piece in this game. Now is your time to move."

"What do you need me to do, sir?" Tony asked with a sly grin.

"Find out who has the diamonds and drugs, then take it. Kill everyone until you find it. Is that too much to remember?"

"I'm on it, Pauly."

The danger radar of the situation was on high with the Sicilian mob boss. Too much was on his plate to be at war with a pathetic street thug that didn't want to cough up a major debt. His earnings were decreasing fast and the fifty million dollars was his only way back on top. The blood in his body began to boil while he thought of Ghost. If blood was what he wanted, the game was on. The time to vacate Brooklyn was already planned in his head and every coin he could get his hands on was going to be swept along when it came.

Chris Green

Chapter 19

Ghost sat quietly in the passenger seat as Jimmie pulled inside the Brooklyn Way Hotel on 4th Avenue.

"Are you sure this is the right place?"

"I'm sure. They said that they're in room one sixteen," Ghost responded, looking at D-Lo and Michael as they pulled in beside them.

Stepping out of the cars, they walked calmly inside the hotel.

"When did they arrive up here? And why we pulling them into this? They should have stayed down in Atlanta," D-Lo whispered, walking next to Ghost.

"Mark and Gunz are true soldiers. It's for sure that we gone need some extra help. They offered and I accepted."

"Fuck getting help. If we start killing a few more motherfuckers then maybe this pussy will let Erica go. We ain't laying no press down."

Ghost listened to his brother as all five of them walked up the steps. "All we gotta do is lay on him and keep striking when the time is right. Rushing shit is what got us in this spot in the first place, D-Lo." Ghost knocked two times on the door before Gunz opened it wide, letting them all in.

"How long do we have to keep playing the same song with this fucking coward?" Jaylen asked as the room door closed.

"That's the same thing I'm trying to figure out," D-Lo cut back.

Ghost shook Mark's and Gunz's hands before he took a seat on the bed. "And I'm trying to see how many times I gotta tell you fucking retards the same thing. We ain't tryna to run headfirst into this shit. We've lost so much already," Ghost spat, tired of hearing D-Lo's mouth.

"If you ask me, we've lost all we can lose. Your son was just killed and your baby mama is probably dead. She's a fucking Fed, Ghost. Why are we even wasting our time?"

Jimmie and Michael leaned against the wall, knowing the debate was about to get out of hand.

"If me saving this girl so that my kids can have a mother is a waste of time, then so be it. No one is begging you to be here. What the fuck is your problem? Ever since we came up here your energy has been fucked up with everyone. Whose side are you on?"

"Listen, me and Chance came up with a plan to end this and get Erica back. All we have to do is follow his lead and move carefully. His face will have to be shown sooner or later," Michael said.

"This shit is funny as fuck. We're obviously losing our touch. We been cooped up in these rooms like pigeons in bird cages. Y'all acting like ya' period on or some shit. Am I the only one that gives a fuck about my nephew being murdered?" D-Lo yelled, looking at everyone in the room.

"Son, you need to relax," Michael said, trying to ease him.

"No, you need to relax. You've been away from us nineteen plus years. This isn't him. The Ghost I know would have unleashed on the whole fucking city. Now we're moving around like a motherfucker got press on us."

"You feel you know everything that needs to happen. You want to be in control so bad, my nigga, go ahead. Tell us what we need to do!"

"I say we pull up everywhere this motherfucker play at. Cut the room for him to move anywhere. This nigga got Erica, and sliding around New York like he's untouchable. Everybody needs to slide out in the morning. It's time to start pulling up on people, asking some questions. It's the only way we gonna end this shit."

"I'm pulling Ashley out of this shit. I'm gonna tell her to meet us back here and send her back to Atlanta. From now on, you run the show since you got this shit figured out, so much." Ghost said, lighting a cigarette.

"Nah, I ain't got it all figured out. But I bet can make somethin' shake faster than you can."

Ghost's words were contained as he walked over by the small kitchen. He wanted to pull his gun out and slap D-Lo back into reality from the small world he was stuck in. He inhaled another puff of the Newport as he listened to his older brother talk.

"Gunz and Mark, y'all slide through every project this nigga Lockz played in. Y'all will have all the info by morning. Pull up on everyone and ask questions about this Pauly. If a nigga even stumble, wet they ass the fuck up. Dad, Jimmie, y'all can slide around the upper Manhattan area and find us some new spots to lay low in. We need to keep it moving daily. Jaylen, you can ride with me. I'm taking us up through the Queen's area and see if a few cats out that way want a lil' chedda to spill some beans on this pasta eating motherfucker."

"I don't think that is a good idea, son," Michael replied cutting in.

"But I do. It's not up to you anymore. Remember, since you been stressing so hard? You and Ghost can take a little day off, if you like."

Ghost shook his head in disgust with D-Lo. His controlling mind frame was beginning to eat at his anger with every word. "Just let him have it, Pop," Ghost said, tapping the ashes of his smoke to the floor.

Michael nodded and leaned against the wall.

"It's simple. Either we mobbing or we starving. We either take care of him or sit around and wait to die."

Ghost tuned D-Lo out as he called Ashley's phone back to back.

"Meet us at the Brooklyn Way hotel," he typed in the phone, sending the message off to her.

She left out of the hotel that morning, searching for any leads that could get them closer to Pauly. The way Ghost was feeling, he was ready to pull away from everyone and handle the business on a personal note.

"Are you sure y'all telling us everything about this? It don't seem like nobody together on this shit," Gunz asked, looking around.

"I think what I just said was clear enough, bruh. Sit back and get y'all some rest. We're heading out in the morning," D-Lo said, walking out of the room.

"Aye, look man, I didn't sign up for this shit. We need to go ahead and take care of this so we can head out. This shit is getting aggravating and overrated," Jaylen spat, walking in circles.

***

Saul and Johnny sat at the card table with a few other people, playing a hand of Blackjack. The only light in the room was the one above their heads. The only noise that came from the mobsters were the poker chips they added up to place their bets.

The knocking on the door interrupted their game. The guard gripped his pistol as he slid the flap on the door back. After seeing Tony's face, he stepped back, letting him in.

"Who the fuck did you think I was? We're the only ones who know about this spot, right? Don't ever take that long to let me in again."

"Tony, how ya' doing, boss? When the hell did you start back gambling?" Saul asked, smiling with the jack and ace of spade in his hand.

"I'm a boss. I don't gamble unless it's with somebody else's shit. I got some business for you and Johnny to handle. Get a few guys, take care of these assholes and get paid."

"What the fuck happened? Did someone fuck with you, Tony?" Saul asked, pulling the gun out of his jacket pocket.

"Calm down, dumbass! Put the fucking gun away. I need you to take care of a few things in the morning. If you make sure it's done correctly, I'll make sure both of ya' are good."

"All you gotta do is point 'em out, Tony. If they gotta go, they gotta go," Johnny said as if the matter was that simple.

"Good. I'll fill you in, in about two hours'. Clean this fucking place up," Tony said, heading back for the door.

"Sure thing, Tony," Saul replied, smiling.

***

The next morning came extra quickly for Ghost. The weed smoke still roamed in the air from the last blunt he rolled. He texted Ashley's phone for the twentieth time, still waiting for a reply. Twenty minutes ago he watched as everyone piled into the cars and left him behind. His eyes watched the screen to see if her name would pop up on the phone.

The vibration startled him, causing his eyes to look at the foreign number that was calling. Pressing the green answer key, he put the phone on speaker.

"You have a pre-paid call from a private detention facility. This call will be recorded and monitored. To accept the call, press five."

Ghost followed the instructions, hitting the button and waited as the call processed.

"Whoa?"

"What the fuck going on, my boy? How you holding up?" Ghost asked, happy to hear from Suave.

"You know they listening, but everything mafioso. Harvey's assistant got me a twenty-five-year plea. I just took that shit and ran with it. Where's Erica?"

"She's around, bro. It's still the same way it was before you left. I'm starting to run out of options. I know it's only so much I can really say, but shit is ugly. I'm gonna make sure you straight in there, fool. I'ma do whatever in my power to get that bid knocked down. Don't stress about none of this shit out here. We gotta keep this shit pushing until we come out on top."

"Facts. You know where my loyalty stands with you, bro. When I get home, it's back to the usual of getting this bread and staying out of sight. Just stay safe out there, bro. It's something I need to let you know. I'm gonna wait till you get settled in a spot, so I can write you a kite."

"Most definitely. Stay omerta, my bro. Sit tight and stay out of trouble."

"Two love, bro."

"Two love, fool," Ghost replied, hanging up.

Standing out of the chair, the answer struck his mind instantly on what to do. He quickly tossed on his shoes, placing a call to D-Lo's phone.

8:00AM

Mark and Gunz pulled slowly inside the parking lot of Pink Houses. They came to a halt directly in front of the three hustlers who were posted up. Gunz rolled down the driver's side window, blowing out a cloud of weed smoke.

"Say there, fellas."

"Yo, what's good, my nigga? Y'all must be lost or something," one of the men replied.

"Nah, we just trying to see if you niggas down with making some paper quick and easy," Gunz said, holding the bundles of hundreds out of the window.

The green rolls of currency instantly grabbed their attention as all three men locked in on the jackpot in Gunz's hand.

"Hell yeah, son! What the fuck you need?"

"I'm just trying to find out something. Have you ever heard of Pauly?" Gunz could tell from the reaction on the man's face that he hit a nerve.

"Nah, cuz. Never heard of him. You might be in the wrong place."

Mark could feel the tension in his words and gripped the handle of his pistol.

Gunz grabbed Mark's wrist, easing him and looked back at the young gangsta. "Say less, shawty."

Rolling the window up, he eased the car into a U-turn and headed back up to the entrance. The black Cadillac that swerved in front of them caused him to slam his foot on the brakes. The three masked men that arose from the vehicle raised their Ak-47s directly to the windshield. Gunz's body froze as the chaos began to erupt.

Bloc! Bloc! Bloc! Bloc! Bloc! Bloc! Bloc! Bloc!

The bullets caved quickly into the glass, striking Gunz in the center of his chest. Mark tried to duck under the seat as the hot lead cut through the thin medal. The bullet that struck his hand forced him to open the door with his other hand and run for it.

Six bullets entered the top of his back, making him fall to the ground. One man walked towards the car, placing another shot into Gunz's skull. Moving to the opposite side he did the same to Mark and walked calmly back to the car.

The people that looked on in horror gathered around as civilians began to jump on their cellphones.

Chapter 20

D-Lo cruised smoothly in the BMW rental. The tint on the car allowed him to scope every corner of Brooklyn as he called his father's phone.

"Hello?"

"Whoa, Pop, head back towards Ghost's way. Me and Jaylen found out some good shit that can end this."

"We're on our way," Michael replied, hanging up.

Placing the phone in his lap, he lit a Newport as he rolled down the window.

"So, do you think that nigga in Queens was serious about that nigga Pauly? How do we know for sure that shit even exist? The Social Butterfly? It doesn't even sound real." Jaylen remarked.

"It's real. I typed it in the GPS on my iPhone. It's over on Atlantic Avenue. The only question is what does Pauly have to do with this club? I'm gonna stop by the old room real quick and get a few straps we left. Then we're heading back over to Ghost. Text Gunz and let them know to go ahead and slide back out that way."

Jaylen nodded quietly as D-Lo turned the volume of the radio to the max. Ghost's number popped on the screen of his phone while he rapped along with the T.I. song that blasted through the speakers.

"You don't wanna see the trigger man bust. Hit you and ya' man's up. Make it hard for niggas to stand up."

By the time the song ended, he never recognized Ghost called his line three times. Pulling down 4th Avenue, he parked on the side curb and jumped out, heading for the room. Jaylen waited inside, bobbing his head from the next song that touched the radio.

Walking up to the door, D-Lo pulled the key out of his pocket, sliding it into the slot. Making his way inside, he walked towards the refrigerator, sliding his hands underneath for the two Glocks. His eyes roamed to the floor of the bathroom across from him. Ashley's detached head laid on the floor, staring directly at him. his eyes began to widen in shock as he slowly stood to his feet and took a few steps forward. He pushed the door open, exposing her shredded body. The blood that was splattered across the floor made his stomach turn as he backed out of the door, and left the room.

Walking outside, his mind was racing. Stepping off the sidewalk, the doors to the parked van slid open. His eyes caught the motion, but his hand reacted too slowly. The blast from the sawed-off shotgun blew a hole through his stomach as he took his next step.

Boom!

His cellphone flew out of his hand, hitting the ground. He gasped harshly searching for his breath, dropping to his knees. The killer walked over to him, aiming his gun.

"Enjoy hell, motherfucker!"

The chrome 45 automatic released, knocking a chunk out the middle of his dreads.

Boc!

Looking to his side, Jaylen spotted the trouble and jumped out the car with his gun blazing.

Boc! Boc! Boc! Boc! Boc! Boc! Boc!

He clapped his gun, maneuvering to the driver's side of the car. The sight of D-Lo's dead body could be seen from where he stood. The sound of the shotgun started to roar, making Jaylen hop inside the car.

Boom! Boom!

The vibration of the whip shook roughly making him put the car in drive and smash off.

35 minutes later

Ghost, Michal and Jimmie sat quietly in the room, waiting for the rest of the crew to return. Jimmie leaned up in his chair, looking at Michael.

"I think something's wrong. We tried calling all of their phones and still haven't gotten an answer. That was almost forty minutes ago."

"It could be anything. We just gotta wait until they call us back. We don't need to just jump to conclusions."

Ghost continued to ignore their words while he repeatedly called D-Lo's number. The banging on the room door caused all of them to grab their weapons in a silent motion.

Michael crept over to the door, looking through the peephole. Stepping back, he opened it up, allowing Jaylen to run in the room.

"What the fuck happened?" Jimmie asked, jumping to his feet.

Jaylen tried his best to catch his breath. The sweat that was running down his face indicated that something was wrong. "We got shot!"

"What! Where in the fuck is my brother, nigga?" Ghost asked, with his chest heaving hard.

"He's dead. They killed him!"

Ghost's heart fell into the pit of his stomach, as the words slid into his ears. Jimmie covered the top of his head, walking towards the bathroom.

"You let my brother die," Ghost whispered as the tears began to well in his eyes.

"It was so fast, bro. I didn't see shit. The bullets just kept hitting the car. He was already gone, Ghost."

His vision began to black out quickly with the rush flowing through his veins.

Michael saw the flash from the bullet that entered into Jaylen's eye, exiting the back of his head. Ghost began to aim the gun recklessly, letting the pain pour out .

"Chance! Put the gun down, son," Michael said calmly, with his hands in the air.

The tears that slid down his face dropped to the floor. Jimmie and Michael stood frozen, watching Ghost fall to his knees in a defeat. "Just tell me I'm dreaming. Tell me my big brother isn't gone, Pop."

Michael looked into the soulless eyes of his son and nodded slowly. Grabbing the back of his head he embraced him in a tight grip. "Please, listen to me. Exploding will do us no justice on this, Chance. I'm sorry, son," Michael said, choking on his own tears.

"Sorry? What the fuck am I gonna do without my brother? I'm nothing without him. That's my other half, dad."

"We're gonna do exactly what he was trying to do. It's time to kill this problem. You even said it yourself. You know what has to be done."

Jimmie walked over to them, placing his hand on Ghost's shoulder. "I know it's nothing I can say to make neither one of you feel any better on this matter. But I'm willing to put my life on the line to catch whoever did this to D-Lo."

"Everybody's disappearing and dying. It's no point of even trying anymore," Ghost mumbled with his head down.

"That's where you are wrong, Chance. This man— his arrogant ways and foolish thinking— is our advantage. It's always a weakness in every plot. We have to go," Michael said with a thirsty look for blood in his eyes.

Ghost sat stuck, looking in his father's face. The world seemed as if it had started moving in slow motion. The same look that he noticed in his own eyes, it was the look of a real killer. Standing to his feet, he slowly placed his gun back on his waist. "I'm ready."

Michael saw the distraught look on his face and knew that Ghost's mind wasn't sitting right. Grabbing the little things they had, Jimmie opened the door and they all headed out into the streets of Brooklyn.

Chris Green

Chapter 21

Beth-Israel Medical Center

The sound of the heart monitor began to slowly raise. Shadow gasped for a large breath of air, making the doctor rush through the door. His eyes began to open, trying to adjust from the blurriness that cloudiness of his pupils. The form of the beautiful white woman began to appear as everything became clear.

"Are you okay, sir?" she asked, with her hand on his chest.

The smell of her Cherry Rose lotion was all he could smell. Her long, black hair hung down her back and her light pink scrubs hugged her thick frame perfectly. Her arched eyebrows and pink lips made her look more like a sexy Playboy bunny instead of a doctor.

"Where in the fuck am I?" Shadow asked, through his dry lips.

"You were shot. You're at Beth Israel's hospital in Brooklyn. I found you laying on the beach," she replied, moving her hands on him to see if it was something else wrong.

"How long have I been here?"

"For five days. You can't be from New York because no family has shown up for you, and we couldn't find any identification on you. Can you tell me your name?"

"I don't know. Why can't I move?" The pace of his heart began to speed again.

"I need you to relax for me. My name is Dr. Thompson. The bullet that hit you in the back, struck a nerve that temporarily paralyzed you. We immediately took you into surgery to remove it. Whoever shot you was two inches away from killing you. That's why I'm trying to find out who you are."

Shadow squeezed his eyes closed, trying to think. His thoughts were so clouded as he tried to take in everything that was going on.

"Do you have any information or a number for a family member?"

"No!"

"Listen, I need you to calm down and get some rest. You're probably experiencing a little memory loss and need to recover a little more."

"If I can't remember a damn thing, what would make me want to take my ass back to bed?" Shadow yelled.

"Nobody knows you're here. This is a private side of the hospital and I'm not leaving out of this room. Can you please just sit back and rest for me?" Doctor Thompson asked with a sincere face.

The medicine that she began to enter inside his IV soothed his muscles instantly. He looked into her beautiful face before his eyes closed. He fell back into a deep sleep.

The Social Butterfly

Michael looked down at his watch, sitting in the driver's seat of the car. They were parked thirty feet away from the club, wanting to spot the right victim. Ghost gripped his pistol tightly while he patiently waited. The slaying of D-Lo made the news and was being broadcasted on every station it could.

To make it worse, the Pink House project shooting fell right behind it. After the camera showed the riddled Camaro on the crime scene, Ghost knew that his friends' fates were sealed. His whole world had crashed down on him within the past few days. Even though his heart ached for his loved ones, the pain made him thirst for Pauly's blood even more.

***

Saul handed Johnny the keys to the car as they walked out of the club. "We have a few more things to take care of and I'll send your half of the loot to you."

"Saul, we've been working three days straight. Don't you think it's time for us to get a break?" Johnny complained, opening the driver's side door.

"We will get a break when Tony tell us to, jackass. This is the way of our life. We work, Johnny. It's just what mobsters do."

Johnny nodded as they climbed in and cranked the vehicle. The dim lights that glowed behind them went unnoticed while he pulled off in the small black Lexus.

Saul used the car lighter to burn the end of his cigar. His eyes drifted to the rearview mirror, looking at the black Challenger that followed behind them. "Get us to the gambling spot to grab a few things. Then we can handle our business."

Looking back into the rearview, Saul could see the car starting to pick up a little speed. He started to say something but was cut off from the car that smashed into them at the four-way split. The small Lexus caved in quickly and began to spin in circles before it came to a halt.

Jimmie stepped out of the F-150 with his Glock 17 ready to kill. He made his way over to Saul and Johnny as Ghost and Michael pulled in beside them. Opening the door to the driver's side, Jimmie struck Johnny in his face with the gun. Michael got out of the car quickly, making his way to the other side.

"Who the fuck are you?" Saul asked in a dizzy slur, looking up at Michael.

The solid punch that landed on his chin put him straight to sleep. Michael dragged him out of the seat toward the trunk of Ghost's car. After throwing Saul inside, he handcuffed his wrist and shut him inside. Jimmie put Johnny over his shoulders and placed him in the back of the truck. Jumping in the cars, they swerved off, heading to a new destination. The time of death was coming and Ghost wanted to make sure he was the last tick that ended it all.

Chapter 22

Greenwood Cemetery
11:48PM

Saul opened his eyes, feeling the major pain that had his brain thumping. The headlights of the cars shone brightly. He watched as the two men threw Johnny face first on the grass.

"Bring that pussy ass nigga over here with him," Ghost spat, looking down at Saul.

Jimmie grabbed Johnny's legs and pulled them, making him hit his head on the hard ground.

"You pricks are gonna be buried with the sewer rats when I finish with you motherfuckers," Johnny ranted as Jimmie placed him on his knees.

Ghost wasted no time kicking him in the mouth for the disrespect. "You stupid clown ass motherfuckers might not understand the situation so clearly, so I'ma brighten it for you." Pulling the hunting knife out of his jacket, he carved it in the side of Johnny's neck. His handgun slid from the waistline, finishing him off with three face shots.

Bloc! Bloc! Bloc!

"Jesus fucking Christ!" Saul yelled, witnessing his partner's soul leave his body.

Jimmie and Michael stood with stone faces while Ghost cleaned the blade of his knife.

"Now that we all understand that this isn't a joke, I want to have a little chat with you."

"Hey, listen big guy, just take it easy. I'll tell you where the stash is. Just don't kill me," Saul pleaded.

Ghost shook his head and picked up the gas can next to the tire. Walking over to Johnny, he began to pour the liquid on top of his face. Pulling out his lighter, he struck

199

Johnny's hair, turning his head into a ball of flames. Saul's mouth sat wide open, staring into Ghost's eyes. He knew that he was about to feel death.

"I'm looking for Pauly. I know that you are gonna come out your mouth with the stupidest shit ever. But I'm still willing to give you a shot at saving yourself. Where is my girl?"

"I swear to fucking God, I don't know what you're talking about. What girl? Pauly barely even speaks to me. I'm just a measly worker," Saul said truthfully.

"Listen, tonight everything you know ends. This conversation, your life and a lot of other shit that's about to crash down on your fucking head. Just tell me where I can find him and you can go free. Please make this shit easy," Ghost said with the rage starting to boil harder.

"You're gonna kill me anyway. How can I guarantee you'll let me live?"

"Time is ticking. That's up to you on wasting this choice. I think you need to make ya' fucking mind up before I change mine."

"We need to go, Chance," Michael said, looking at Johnny's body covered in flames.

Saul sweat profusely trying to gain his thoughts. "Two hundred east ninety-fourth street, number nine sixteen. That's where you can find him."

"All this running around we doing. How the fuck do we know you telling the truth, sleazy ass rat?" Jimmie asked, sick of the chasing game.

"Hey buddy, you asked me and I told ya'. There's nothing else I can tell you!"

"Fair enough. Pop, let him go," Ghost said nodding towards him.

"Are you sure?"

"I'm sure."

Michael walked over to Saul, placing the key inside of the handcuffs. After releasing them, he walked back to Ghost's side.

Saul stood to his feet, looking Ghost in his eyes. "You did the right thing, kid. You won't regret it."

Ghost flashed a sly smile, pointing the Ruger at his leg, Releasing one shot.

"Ahh! Damn it! You fuckingg bastard!" He howled in pain.

"The only reason I'm not going to kill you is because you're too stupid to realize what you're getting yourself into. Do yourself a favor and stay far away from this situation. Do you hear me?"

"Yes, I understand."

"Let's go," Ghost mumbled, walking past Michael and Jimmie.

Getting back inside their cars, they pulled out of Greenwood cemetery, leaving their trail of blood behind.

"Are you ready to handle this?" Michael asked, sitting in he passenger seat.

Ghost shook his head. "I want to catch him tomorrow. I don't want any mistakes. All we have to do is keep this plan together. It's no way for him to hide anymore."

"We gotta use our heads on this. I want ya' to now I'm moving with you, Chance. No matter how downhill it goes, I'm gonna die by your side. My son is dead because of me, and your child's mother and son is gone for the mistakes I made."

"Dad! The time for blaming yourself is done and over. This man made the choice to cause harm to our family. No matter what the situation was. Now is the time for us to make him feel our pain."

Michael soaked in the words from his son while he cruised to the speed limit.

Aloft Harlem Hotel
2:00 am

Ghost sat on the edge of the bed in his hotel room looking out at the night sky. He inhaled hard on the blunt, letting the smoke cloud the center of his chest. So many losses were issued on this journey for him. D-Lo's face continued to pop into his mind, making his eyes close. The glimpse of his son flashed as he stood to his feet. Picking up his cellphone, he dialed a number and placed it up to his ear.

"Hello?"

"I love you," Ghost said, happy to hear her beautiful voice.

"I love you too, Chance," Tiffany replied.

"Do you like the house?"

"Yes, Chance, but I would love it if you would come home and enjoy it with me."

"I will, Tiff, I promise," Ghost whispered, hearing the hurt deep in her voice.

Hearing the phone hang up in his face, he placed it back on the bed. The flashy lights of New York City shone bright while Ghost walked over to the window. The air from the cold breeze slid across his face as he took a deep breath. Even though he stood in that spot, his soul felt like it didn't even exist. In a few months, he practically lost everybody close to him. For some reason he felt that his grave was coming soon.

***

It was the next morning when Ghost stood in the bathroom, observing himself in the mirror. Putting his gun on his waistline, he fixed the collar to his black Armani shirt before leaving.

"Are you ready?" Michael asked, looking at Ghost come out of the restroom.

"Yeah, we can go now."

"Are you sure you want to go into this place on your own, Ghost? I mean how are you gonna even get inside?" Jimmie asked, feeling something bad could occur.

"I'm sure. I've made my way through shit like this time after time. I'm gonna find a way to get inside. Just make sure the earpiece I gave you is working. If you hear something wrong, then you know what to do."

"It's ten o'clock in the morning. Do you think this dude is actually at home?"

"It wouldn't matter. I'm not leaving until I take care of it. Stick around the perimeter, in case something seems shady. Besides that, I can handle the rest on my own."

"Just make sure you keep the phone going so I can hear the conversation. I don't wanna lose a connection with you," Michael replied, opening the room door.

After the understanding was made, they headed out, preparing to end the storm that rained for so long.

Chris Green

Chapter 23

Carnegie Park Condominiums

As Michael pulled the car down 200 East 94 Street, he stopped in front of the thirty-story building.

"They have security at the front desk. Try and stay unnoticed."

"I got it, Pop," Ghost said, looking at him and Jimmie with a straight face.

Steeping out of the backseat, he closed the car door and headed inside the condominiums.

The floor to the entrance shone brightly. Ghost made his way quickly across the lobby while the security held the attention of a blonde-haired woman. Keeping his head low from the camera, he walked into the pathway, pressing the button to the elevator. He waited patiently until the doors slid gently open. Stepping inside, he pressed the number nine as his eyes roamed around the corners of the walls while the doors closed.

Moving quickly, Ghost pulled out his silenced handgun and checked the chamber.

"Can y'all hear me? I'm in," Ghost mumbled into the earpiece.

"We can hear you just fine. We're gonna keep circling the area in case we can spot 'em. He's not gonna be alone. So be careful," Michael replied.

Ghost humbled himself as the doors opened up. He made his way onto the walkway, looking at the numbers on the doors while he breezed past. Stopping in front of room nine sixteen, he looked at the keycard slot. He tapped on the door four times to see if he could hear any movement. Nothing but silence came from inside. He listened carefully, grabbing onto the handle of the door.

"Is there something I can help you with, sir?"

Ghost snapped his head around, looking at the old, white housekeeper.

"Yes, ma'am, I've seemed to have locked myself out of my room. The darn kids took the keycard and lost it. Now my wife is pulling a flipper on me because I left her luggage on the bed."

"It's okay, sir. I'll be glad to help you out." Walking in front of him, she pulled out her master keycard and opened up the apartment.

Ghost pulled his weapon before she could turn back around. "Now step in."

The fear from the gun made her step in as Ghost followed, closing the door behind him.

***

The black Mercedes-Benz pulled in front of the condominiums, stopping at the curb. Pauly stepped out of the vehicle with his three bodyguards on his tail.

"Hey, listen, all of you have been through a rough week. Tomorrow is a big day. After these Africans are taken care of, we will proceed to normal business again. Go home and get some rest."

"Are you sure, Pauly? Don't you think we should try and end this issue?" Tony asked with a serious tone.

"I said that we rest today. Things will be handled. Let the guys take a night off to be with their families. We're the ones running the show on this move, Tony. It's no need to rush."

"Whatever you say, boss. Come on, fellas."

Pauly headed inside of the building while his crew got back into the car and pulled off. His shoes tapped against the tile floors, heading for the entrance.

"Pauly! How ya' doing, big guy?" the security asked, standing guard in front of the check-in booth.

Nodding, he continued to walk and slide inside the open elevator, pressing the button to his level. He loosened his tie and leaned up on the wall until the bell notified him of his floor.

Pauly stepped out into the breezeway of his unit and headed for his door. Pulling the card out his pocket, he slid it inside and walked in. Closing the door behind him, he slid on the latch and turned the bottom lock. Turning around, he placed his trench coat on the rack, with his pistol still inside.

Making his way to the black mini bar, he grabbed one of his cigars and sparked it with the blue flame of his chrome lighter. He paused, looking at the open bottle of Remy Martin.

"This is a nice place you got here."

Pauly looked over at Ghost sitting in the seat of his Italian leather chair. The pistol that was in his hand was aimed stiffly, while he finished off the last of his liquor.

"How the fuck did you get into my place?"

Ghost pointed at the old woman who sat in the corner with her hands and mouth taped. "Sit the fuck down!"

Pauly released the cigar smoke and cracked a little smile, nodding. Making his way to the chair across from Ghost, he smiled at him evilly. "You know this is not gonna end well, right?" Pauly asked, sitting down, crossing his leg. He puffed on the cigar while they looked into each other's eyes.

"Yeah, I know. And that's the reason I'm gonna give you a chance to resolve things easily so this little problem will go away."

The light chuckle that Pauly released made Ghost's jaw clench. "You know something? You're a very admirable person. You're strong-minded, you have the maturity of a wise guy like myself, you absorb things quickly, and I'm sure that you measured your time to make this little meeting occur. But I think we still have a little unfinished business to handle."

Ghost placed his cellphone on the center part of the table while he mugged Pauly. "You murdered my son, you had my brother and some of the closest people to me killed for your own certain reasons. You took my child's mother away from us and you tell me we have unfinished business?"

"And your father stole fifty million dollars of my fucking diamonds. Pure fucking diamonds. That was twenty years ago. The drama and chaos I've gone through to get those jewels back has caused me my wife's life, my mother and even the cold-hearted bastard I called my father."

"Unfortunately, I don't give a fuck about your father. I don't care about your diamonds. I care that you made the worst mistake of your life by harming my family," Ghost said, lighting his cigarette.

"If you kill me, you will never find your little girlfriend. That's the reason you are here, right, for her? She's already halfway dead, but she's still alive. You can have her and return my drugs and stones. We can call it even and continue on with our lives?"

"How about you just tell me where the fuck she is before I put a bullet in your head?"

"Do you like Italian food? When I was younger I always used to help my mom when she was in the kitchen, for some reason. My father didn't like that. He felt that it was always a woman's job to handle those types of things. I knew that it was my dream to make the best Italian food. I enjoy doing it."

Ghost held the pistol in his hand as he listened to Pauly rant.

"My point is, I followed the way I wanted to go and it was a dream come true. We all have to make a choice one day. You have to make yours also."

***

Michael and Jimmie sat quietly listening to every word that was being said. Hearing they key word Italian made the lightbulb click into Michael's head as he looked at Jimmie.

"Did you just hear that?"

"Hear what?"

"Did you hear what Pauly just said?" Michael repeated with a serious face.

"What? About making a choice?"

"No, that he loves to make Italian food. Have you ever wondered why we never could catch him anywhere?"

"Not really."

"I think I know where Erica is," Michael said, cranking the car up.

"Where?"

Michael ignored him as he spoke through the earpiece. "Chance, don't kill him. I think I know where he's hiding her!"

Swerving out into the street, he mashed the gas, heading in the opposite direction.

***

Ghost kept a blank face when hearing Michael speak. The thought of finding Erica made his heartrate fluctuate. "My choice was made when you forced my hand on doing this. What kind of deal was it that you made with Jesus? Because it couldn't have been worth you getting your ass blown away today."

"Oh, I think it is. I don't know if your little brain can remember that far back, but take a whiff, son. Your father's supposed to be in a box. He's the one that caused this madness to happen and unfold. Instead of being loyal to Jesus, he turned into a fucking snake. Let me explain something to you. One rotten apple can spoil a whole batch of good, loyal men. You have to know how to divide the weak from the solid," Pauly said, inhaling his cigar again.

Ghost kept his eyes pierced on him, sitting quietly.

"You type of people don't know what the fuck solid is about. Everything we strive for is earned. You ain't never put any work in. You have people go and do your dirty work for you, and try to take all the credit."

"No! I make the dirty work."

"You make problems that you can't handle. If you really knew who you were fucking with, you would have left this entire situation alone. All I want is my diamonds and my drugs. What type of man do you feel that you are? You think you can just take something that belongs to me and I'm supposed to walk away? My people want my blood for this mishap. You, as a man, should know what that feels like if you're running an operation, like you say you are."

Ghost continued to listen to Michael whisper in his ear while he stared at Pauly.

Chapter 24

Michael sweated bullets while he focused on speeding through the traffic that was out.

"Yo, you need to slow the fuck down. How the fuck are you just so sure that she's there?" Jimmie asked, paranoid that the police could get on their tail.

"It's the last option we have right now. We have to try." He slowed the car down as he turned on 236 West 56 Street. Parking at the end of the sidewalk, he looked over at Jimmie.

"Are you really serious, Michael? This is a big risk going in a fucking restaurant. It may be tons of innocent people in there, who can point us out. Ghost needs us right now."

"And we need this to end. I need you to trust me on this." Michael nodded with a sure expression.

Pulling the two Glocks from his hip, he checked them and shook his head. "If we go out bad, just know you're the reason."

"All I need you to do is stand by the door and don't let anyone out. Pull the trigger if you have to."

After looking at Patsy's restaurant, they looked at each other and jumped out the car.

***

Ghost kept his ear tuned in to everything Michael was saying. The bad feeling he had in his heart made him want to stop them. But before he could, the first gunshot rang in his ear loudly.

"Get the fuck up! Go to the balcony. Now!" Ghost yelled, pointing the pistol at Pauly's head.

Pauly raised out of his chair with an amused smile. "You know you want to see that girl alive again. You can't kill me, Ghost."

Slapping him in the back of the head while he walked, Ghost grabbed the collar of his shirt and pushed him outside on the patio.

Pauly stumbled and looked back at Ghost with an evil grin. "You're all gonna die!"

***

Michael moved quickly, making his way into the front door of the restaurant with Jimmie on his heels. The sound of the front door slamming and locking snatched everyone's attention. Seeing the guns, everyone began to scream and duck as Michael moved towards the tables. Two men that came from the kitchen in black suits was all it took for him to start war.

He placed one shot to a guard's skull while they tried to pull their weapons.

Boc!

The next bullet quickly landed in the second man's chest, making him drop to the floor.

"All y'all stay the fuck down and shut the fuck up," Jimmie yelled.

Michael held his gun with precision and slowly walked into the kitchen. The workers and chefs got on the floor as he opened every freezer, looking inside. His mind was in overdrive when making his way back out. The flight of steps that sat by the end table caught his attention. He slowly made his way up the steps with his gun leading. When he put his foot on the last step, the gunfire that came from around the corner made him jump back.

Placing his arm around the wall, he began to empty more shots.

Boc! Boc! Boc! Boc!

Hearing the body crash to the floor, he made his way around the corner with his pistol ready to burst again.

The man laid with his chest open against the solid, thick, white door. Moving swiftly, Michael stepped over the guard and eyed the keyhole at the top right corner. He placed his body towards the room and leveled his shoulder. Counting to two, he jumped against the door and bounced back off. The pain that erupted through his shoulder told him that it wasn't the usual cheap wood he was used to getting through.

Looking down at the guard, he began to search his pockets quickly and discovered the big silver key that he needed. Placing it in the lock, he turned it and pushed the door with his gun in hand.

Freezing in his tracks, he stared at Erica, laid against the concrete wall. Rushing to her side, he lifted her head, lightly tapping her. Erica slowly opened her red eyes, staring at him.

"Please, help me," she said barely above a whisper.

Michael pulled the keys to the handcuffs from his pocket and released the latches from around her. Her scarred wrists were swollen and the dried blood that was on her legs was a clear sign that she was raped. Taking off his long sleeve white shirt, he wrapped it around her body and picked her up, walking out of the room. He made his way back through the hallway and down the steps.

Jimmie continued to keep his two guns aimed as Michael came down the stairs with her in his arms. He instantly made his way towards them, staring down at her.

"Oh my God, you found her," Jimmie whispered.

Michael nodded while he carried her out the restaurant and back to the car.

"Chance, we got her. It's over. She's hurt very bad, but I got her," Michael said into his earpiece as him and Jimmie got in the car and swerved off.

Ghost's heart dropped when he heard his father speak in his ear. "You took me through a lot to get up here and make you release my woman. My family died in vain because your pride was in the way on being a boss."

"All you have to do is return what belongs to me and you can have her back," Pauly ranted as the sun beamed down on him. The laugh that came from Ghost made his heart beat faster.

"Stupid ass Italian. It wasn't that hard. But I applaud you for trying. You are asking for shit that doesn't belong to you anymore. Those diamonds are mine. The two hundred kilos of coke is mine. I got my woman out of your restaurant a few seconds ago. Because she's mine."

Pauly flipped his hand through his hair with a destroyed look. His smile turned to a sinister mug as he tried to rush Ghost. The first shot to his shoulder knocked him back to the edge of the balcony wall.

Boc!

"Arghhh!"

He wasted no time letting him have another two hollow tips to his head.

Boc! Boc!

His body pushed back, flipping off of the eighth-floor rail. Ghost looked over the wall as his body crashed into a Yellow taxi that was parked at the ground floor.

Placing his gun on his waist, he made his way back inside the apartment. Walking over to the housekeeping lady, he pulled his knife from his pocket and bent down in front of her. The woman closed her eyes and jerked when Ghost cut the tape off of her wrist. Pulling the tape from her mouth, she began to breathe harder.

"I'm not gonna hurt you. You don't remember nothing you seen here today, understand?"

"Yes, I promise. I won't say anything."

"Are you sure?"

"I don't know what you're talking about, sir."

"Good girl. I want you to take this and go enjoy the rest of your life," Ghost said, dropping a diamond in the center of her palm.

Staring at the diamond in amazement, she lifted her head and looked at Ghost with a wide mouth.

"That's worth one million dollars. Find someone who can cash you out for it and I'll promise you won't be disappointed."

"Thank you, sir."

Ghost winked as he walked out of the room quickly. After getting on the elevator, he made his way downstairs to the main lobby. The crowd that stood around the front of the building was the distraction he needed to get out unnoticed. The police cruisers and ambulances made their way in front of the building. Ghost hopped in the back of a cab and handed the driver a hundred-dollar bill.

"Where to, sir?"

"Just pull off now. As you drive, I'll let you know."

Chris Green

Chapter 25

30 minutes later

Pulling into the small private air strip in Queens, Ghost stepped out of the car and tipped the driver before he pulled off. Pulling out his cell, he placed the call to Michael and waited for an answer.

"We're almost there. We made a small stop. But no more than five or ten minutes away."

"I'm already here. I need you to hurry up, Pop. We have to get out of the states now."

"I'll see you in a second."

Hanging up, Ghost made his way over to the man that was posted by the white jet. "Did you get the info we asked for?"

Pulling an envelope out of his leather coat, he stared at Ghost, placing it in his hand. "I'm supposed to receive half of the cash up-front. That was the agreement, right?"

"What's understood doesn't have to be explained. You will get forty thousand now and forty thousand when we land. How fast do you think we can get there?"

"We gotta try to stay off the radar in the sky. I can only go so high in the air. It'll take us about five and a half, six hours at the most, to land."

"All I need for you to do is get us there and all the rest is good."

"Everything is good, far as I can see. We can get in the air whenever you are ready," the man replied, getting on the plane.

The feeling that was in Ghost's stomach made him ready to leave. The only thing that continued to pain him was the loss of D-Lo and Bernard. He knew the hardest part was gonna be telling Erica that her son was gone.

Rubbing his hand through his hair, he took a deep breath as Michael pulled into the lot. Making his way to the car, he opened the back door. Michael and Jimmie stepped out while Ghost pulled Erica up from the backseat. His heart crumbled even harder looking at her face. Her swollen eyes began to slightly open.

"I knew you would come for me," she mumbled.

His tears couldn't help but fall down his cheek when holding her in his arms.

Jimmie began to rush, grabbing the duffel bags out of the car. Making their way to the plane, Ghost strapped her down in a seat and adjusted the notches to lay her back.

"Are you okay?" Michael asked Ghost, touching his shoulder.

"Yeah, I can't believe you found her. How did you know she was there?"

"He gave himself away. It wasn't about the things he did, it was the messages he left and said. Pauly is a cook, when he isn't handling business. He's either eating or cooking Italian food. Patsy's is a family owned restaurant that he happens to be in charge of. What better place to keep a hostage? A place where he's comfortable; one that he might even love."

Ghost nodded as he stared at Erica.

"Are you guys ready for takeoff?" the pilot asked, stepping in the passenger area of the jet.

"We can leave now. Get us there as quickly as possible," Michael replied, handing the man a yellow manila folder.

"Right away. Everybody strap in and prepare for takeoff. I'll radio when we are about to land."

Sitting in their seats, the engine to the plane came to life. Michael looked over at Ghost taking the seat next to

Erica. "This situation is gonna weigh heavy on our movements, Chance. Pauly's people won't respect his death. I know we have taken a lot of sacrifices and losses, but now is the time to stay clear from these people."

"I'm listening to you, Pop. I just wanna take it one step at a time and get out of here first."

Nodding, Michael sat back in his seat as the plane took off in the air. Closing his eyes, he envisioned all the blood that was spilled, and all the lives that were taken. His heart was ready to rest, but his mind told him that the deaths were far from over.

2 days later
Virgin Islands

Tiffany cracked her eyes when the light of the sun crossed her face. The smell of the beach ran through her nose when she lifted her arms to stretch. Climbing out the bed, she made her way across the soft carpet and headed downstairs. Ghost sat at the table while Jimmie prepared himself to leave.

"Damn, I guess ya' finally came to at least say hey to ya' big brother," he joked, seeing her walk into the dining space.

"It's nothing personal. I've been sticking to myself and staying quiet towards everybody," she replied, looking down at Ghost.

"Well, for what it's worth, I'm glad you're safe. This is a new feeling and a better start for you. I'll be sure to ring y'all line when I make it back." Kissing the top of her forehead, Jimmie nodded at Ghost and walked out.

"So, how is she doing?" Tiffany asked, taking a seat in front of Ghost.

"She needs rest. Her head isn't right, just yet. I've tried talking to her and she won't say anything to me."

"Have you told her?"

"Yes, Tiffany, I had to tell her."

"So, what are you gonna do about it?"

"It's nothing we can do, Tiff."

"Bullshit. They killed half of our family, Ghost. You seen the messages. It's only a matter of time before someone finds out where our home is and harms us again. Don't you think we need to handle this? They killed my stepson and your brother," Tiffany whispered with a disgusted face.

"So what the fuck do you want me to do, Tiffany? You want me to go and kill everybody? Huh? You know how my dad is feeling about this situation."

"Fuck him! When did we let somebody else come and control our fucking family? Ever since he's been around, you've changed. You aren't being yourself, Chance. I'm asking you to open your eyes and realize what is going on." Getting up from the table, Tiffany headed back up the stairs, leaving Ghost to himself.

Standing up, he made his way across the floor of the living room. He crossed into the large hallway and stopped in front of the tall oak door. Turning the knob, he walked in.

Erica was sitting up on the bed with Bernard's urn in her hands. Her eyes were swollen and black, and her wristd were still dark red from the bruises.

The female nurse closed the glass door to the large porch area and walked over to Ghost. "I've tried to tell her she needs rest. Her blood pressure isn't normal. Her body has to heal. She's not doing quite good on hearing that right now."

"It's okay, Shanti, let me have a second with her. You can take a break," Ghost said, looking at Erica.

"Sure."

Ghost walked over to the edge of the bed and sat down by the bottom of Erica's feet. He moved closer, sliding the frizzled hair away from her face. Raising her chin, he looked into her dark brown eyes. "I know it hurts, ma. I know the pain you're feeling right now hurts more than anything you've ever felt. I promise that everything is gonna be okay."

"Are you gonna bring my baby back?"

Ghost took a deep breath hearing her words. "Ma, you know I can't do that."

"So why are you talking to me?"

"I'm trying to support you. I know you've been through a lot and I know losing our son is something that will never be able to sit right with you. But you gotta let him rest. Now is not the time to be against each other."

"Do you love me?" Erica asked, tilting her head.

"You know I do."

"Ever since I first met you, I knew that we would spend the rest of our lives together. I used to dream of the day when we would have our own family and move to a place that would always shine. When I gave you my body, I let you become one with me to make that dream a reality. But now my reality has become my nightmare."

Ghost stared her deeply in the eyes as she wiped her tears.

"I've given up my career, I've lost my son and shed blood for this family. We've lost the same people who I grew to call my own brothers. I've killed to be a part of this family and make sure we could still hold our own dream together. So as your family and your woman, I'll ask you again. Do you love me?"

"Yes, I love you."

"I want everybody that had something to do with this dead. Kill their kids, make their loved ones feel the same that your child's mother is feeling right now."

Nodding, Ghost stood up and walked out of the room. Erica continued to rub the top of the urn, thinking to herself. Regardless of where things led, she was going to get revenge for her son, no matter how long it took.

Chapter 26

Six years later

Ghost pulled his car inside the massive driveway of his Virgin Island home. The smell of Magen's Bay Beach roamed in the air as he stepped out of the driver's side.

"Hey, Daddy," Laylah said, sitting on the front porch with the laptop in her lap.

"Hi, beautiful. Where is your sister?"

"She's in the house with Erica and Mama."

"What are you doing out here by yourself?"

"Pa-pa told me that if I study math, he would take me swimming this weekend."

"Sweetie, it's nine o'clock in the morning and it's extremely hot out here. Why don't you come in the house and do that?"

"I'm okay, Daddy."

Ghost smiled, shaking his head at Laylah and walked through the front door of the house, making his way to the living room. Tiffany sat quietly on the couch with the blunt of marijuana burning in between her fingers. Michael sat in the sofa chair across from her, scrolling through the contents of his cellphone.

"Are you okay?" Ghost asked, kissing Tiffany on her right cheek.

"My brother is dead and my niece is with a piece of shit ass bitch who isn't fit to have her." Tiffany said with a hurt look on her face.

"It's fucked up what happened to Jimmie. I was with his daughter most of the night. I even tried to bribe the bitch with money to let me bring her back. The police gave her custody. It's really nothing we can do."

"Oh, it's something that we can do," Tiffany spat with a hurt face.

"Just try to relax. If you give me a little time to finish this problem for Erica, I will go and get her myself, willingly or forcefully."

"Ghost, you have been running around, gunning at these people for the past six years. It's not gonna bring Bernard back."

"I understand that. But her heart hasn't been right ever since. Both of y'all going through a lot, but y'all running me wild with these situations, Tiff."

"I never told you to go for me. You know I can go and handle any problem with whoever causes one. You treat me like I'ma kid and I'm your wife. How about you let me handle my own beef for a change? My gun bust just like yours do," Tiffany spat.

"It's not about any of that bullshit you pumping up in yo' head. You're not leaving off this fucking island. I've risked everything I could to keep y'all safe. And that's what it is."

"You think Erica is the only one who can walk around here and not pay your ass no mind. Watch this!" Tiffany said, heading out the living room as Michael walked in.

"What's going on?" he asked, looking at Ghost with a raised eyebrow.

"She's on a rampage about getting revenge for her brother. It's nothing that I can even do. I don't know who did it. I tried to bring the little girl back with me and the woman said she didn't feel comfortable. Her two nephews are in prison, so the child is basically stuck if she won't give her to me. I don't even really have time for this. I gotta handle something in the A real quick. When I'm finished there, I'll make my way over to snatch the kid and bring her back with me."

"Chance, it's been six years and you're still risking us by going back to Atlanta. You could get hurt."

"Well, guess what? It doesn't even matter anymore. I've tried to move on and let our past stay behind us. Over the past few years, Tiffany and Erica's mind has gotten to be so power-struck that they don't even seem like the same women I fell in love with. You have to know one thing that I'm never gonna change. The way I love my family and the things I would do to keep them safe."

"You need to let me come with you. You always think that you can handle stuff on your own. You feel that you got the world under control from the pull of your trigger, and that's a lie. It always ends somewhere, Chance. Just let me help you."

"I'm sorry, Pop. But no can do," Ghost said, walking up the steps to the master bedroom.

Making his way through the door, he could see Erica's hair that blew in the breeze from the large glass window. Grabbing her by the waist, Ghost kissed the side of her neck softly.

Removing his hands, she spun around and folded her arms across her chest. "I'm not happy right now," Erica said, walking on the other side of the bed to sit down.

"You ain't ever fucking happy. Another morning waking on this earth is enough reason to," he responded.

"Yeah, I bet my son feels the same way, too, huh?"

"Yeah, he does. In the past six years, I've lost my best friend, my brother, my son and plenty more. I've tried to maintain hold of this family and keep us all as safe as possible. But this is who we are, Erica."

"My son wouldn't want to be stuck on a fucking is-land."

"Well, it's a little different now. We can't stay in At-lanta. I'm only going to handle business and I'm out of there. We've started a foundation down here. We can't just up and leave it."

"Yeah. Your way. Always your way," Erica said, put-ting the earbuds to her cellphone in.

Walking off to the giant closet, he went inside, chang-ing his pants and shoes. He grabbed his fake ID and the small pouch that carried the last four diamonds. After put-ting on a fresh tee shirt, he made his way out of the room and headed for the front door.

"Chance, are you sure everything is okay?" Michael asked, catching up to him.

"I already told you, yes. I'm not going up here to play around. I'm handling the business and coming right back."

Opening the door, Ghost walked outside to his car. Starting it up, he backed out of the driveway and cruised off smoothly. Michael dialed a quick number into his phone and place it to his ear.

"What is the reason for this call?" the man answered in an angry voice.

"This is Michael. I may need your help."

"Michael, what have you done now?"

"It's not me, it's my son. He's gonna be getting off a plane at the airport within seven hours in Atlanta."

"And?"

"Follow him to make sure he is good. I need a pair of eyes on him until he comes back."

The man on the phone grew quiet for a second before he spoke. "I'll look into it."

Michael silently nodded and hung up the phone, placing it back in his pocket. He exhaled deeply before walking outside on the porch with Laylah.

Chris Green

Chapter 27

Atlanta, Ga.
Seven hours later

Ghost walked calmly out of the airport doors. He tossed the Louis Vuitton backpack across his shoulder as he made his way towards the parked rental car. Pulling out the keys, he deactivated the alarm and climbed in the front seat. Before he could crank the car, the door swung open with a man shoving the AR-15 in Ghost's face. The loud eruption blasted through his ears as the bullet ripped through his thigh.

"Aghhh!" Ghost grunted, reaching for the pistol in the middle console.

The second feeling was the handle of the gun crashing into the back of his head, knocking him unconscious.

Pushing him over to the backseat, one man jumped in the driver's seat, while the second got back in the getaway car. Swerving out of the parking lot, the white Impala that sat across from the two cars followed them out slowly.

***

"Hey there, tough guy," the Spanish man spoke, pulling the rope around Ghost's feet tighter.

The pressure that thumped in his leg felt as if the Titanic was sitting on top of it. He looked around at the raggedy walls of the small warehouse after catching the pace of his fast beating heart.

"Well, look who decided to join us. Wakey, wakey, motherfucker."

Ghost looked at the two men who beamed over him.

"I'm guessing you already know the reason you're here, right?" the short kidnapper asked.

Removing the pocketknife, he sliced from Ghost's cheek, down to the bottom of his neck. He shook violently, trying to shake the pain of the sharp steel. He began to breathe harshly when the man pulled the blade out of his skin. The alcohol that he began to splash on him turned his wound into an open fire.

"Arghhh! Fuck!"

"Why are you sitting here still playing with this guy? Can we speed up this process, so we can get back to California?" the second kidnapper questioned.

"Hey, shut the fuck up! She put me in charge of this shit. I'm just having a little fun. Just make sure the acid is ready to get rid of this piece of shit."

"I hate that you came all this way for this to happen to you, vato. Eva wants me to send you her greatest love."

Ghost felt his energy getting lower, trying to keep his head up. The bullet that tore through his arm next made him gasp for air.

Boc!

"I need you fully awake during your death, punta. This is what I'm getting paid for."

The tears slightly appeared in his vision as the man pointed the gun to the center of his head.

"You rest easy in hell now, ya' hear me?"

The crashing of the front door is what started the gunfire to erupt.

Boc! Boc! Boc! Boc! Boc!

The killer bumped into Ghost, making the chair fall over. Hitting his head on the ground, the white light began to appear as the gunshots rang through his ear. His heart began to pump slower as the room started to spin.

The gunshots ceased.

The huge Black man moved forward, kicking the gun out of the two dead men's area. After making sure their pulse was gone, he walked over to Ghost. "You're coming with me," was all Ghost heard before everything went black.

The end...
For now!

Stay Connected with Us!

Text **LOCKDOWN** to 22828 to stay
up-to-date with new releases, sneak peaks,
contests and more…

Thank you!

Submission Guideline.

Submit the first three chapters of your completed manuscript to ldpsubmissions@gmail.com, subject line: Your book's title. The manuscript must be in a .doc file and sent as an attachment. Document should be in Times New Roman, double spaced and in size 12 font. Also, provide your synopsis and full contact information. If sending multiple submissions, they must each be in a separate email.

Have a story but no way to send it electronically? You can still submit to LDP/Ca$h Presents. Send in the first three chapters, written or typed, of your completed manuscript to:

LDP: Submissions Dept
Po Box 870494
Mesquite, Tx 75187

DO NOT send original manuscript. Must be a duplicate.

Provide your synopsis and a cover letter containing your full contact information.

Thanks for considering LDP and Ca$h Presents.

Chris Green

BOW DOWN TO MY GANGSTA

By **Ca$h**

TORN BETWEEN TWO

By **Coffee**

BLOOD STAINS OF A SHOTTA **II**

By **Jamaica**

WHEN THE STREETS CLAP BACK **II**

By **Jibril Williams**

STEADY MOBBIN

By **Marcellus Allen**

BLOOD OF A BOSS **V**

By **Askari**

BRIDE OF A HUSTLA **III**

By **Destiny Skai**

WHEN A GOOD GIRL GOES BAD **II**

By **Adrienne**

LOVE & CHASIN' PAPER **II**

By **Qay Crockett**

THE HEART OF A GANGSTA **III**

By **Jerry Jackson**

LOYAL TO THE GAME **IV**

By **T.J. & Jelissa**

A DOPEBOY'S PRAYER **II**

True Savage 3

By **Eddie "Wolf" Lee**

IF LOVING YOU IS WRONG... **III**

By **Jelissa**

BLOODY COMMAS **III**

SKI MASK CARTEL II

By **T.J. Edwards**

BLAST FOR ME **II**

RAISED AS A GOON V

BRED BY THE SLUMS

By **Ghost**

A DISTINGUISHED THUG STOLE MY HEART **III**

By **Meesha**

ADDICTIED TO THE DRAMA **II**

By **Jamila Mathis**

LIPSTICK KILLAH II

By **Mimi**

THE BOSSMAN'S DAUGHTERS 4

By **Aryanna**

Available Now

RESTRAINING ORDER **I & II**

By **CA$H & Coffee**

LOVE KNOWS NO BOUNDARIES **I II & III**

By **Coffee**

RAISED AS A GOON I, II, III & IV

Chris Green

By **Ghost**

LAY IT DOWN **I & II**

LAST OF A DYING BREED

BLOOD STAINS OF A SHOTTA

By **Jamaica**

LOYAL TO THE GAME

LOYAL TO THE GAME II

LOYAL TO THE GAME III

By **TJ & Jelissa**

BLOODY COMMAS I & II

SKI MASK CARTEL

By **T.J. Edwards**

IF LOVING HIM IS WRONG...I & II

By **Jelissa**

WHEN THE STREETS CLAP BACK

By **Jibril Williams**

A DISTINGUISHED THUG STOLE MY HEART I & II

By **Meesha**

PUSH IT TO THE LIMIT

By **Bre' Hayes**

BLOOD OF A BOSS **I, II, III & IV**

By **Askari**

THE STREETS BLEED MURDER **I, II & III**

THE HEART OF A GANGSTA I & II

By **Jerry Jackson**

CUM FOR ME

CUM FOR ME 2

CUM FOR ME 3

An **LDP Erotica Collaboration**

BRIDE OF A HUSTLA **I & II**

THE FETTI GIRLS **I, II& III**

By **Destiny Skai**

WHEN A GOOD GIRL GOES BAD

By **Adrienne**

A GANGSTER'S REVENGE **I II III & IV**

THE BOSS MAN'S DAUGHTERS

THE BOSS MAN'S DAUGHTERS II

THE BOSSMAN'S DAUGHTERS III

A SAVAGE LOVE **I & II**

BAE BELONGS TO ME

A HUSTLER'S DECEIT I, II

By **Aryanna**

A KINGPIN'S AMBITON

A KINGPIN'S AMBITION **II**

I MURDER FOR THE DOUGH

By **Ambitious**

TRUE SAVAGE

TRUE SAVAGE II

TRUE SAVAGE **III**

By **Chris Green**

Chris Green

A DOPEBOY'S PRAYER

By **Eddie "Wolf" Lee**

THE KING CARTEL **I, II & III**

By **Frank Gresham**

THESE NIGGAS AIN'T LOYAL **I, II & III**

By **Nikki Tee**

GANGSTA SHYT **I II &III**

By **CATO**

THE ULTIMATE BETRAYAL

By **Phoenix**

BOSS'N UP **I , II & III**

By **Royal Nicole**

I LOVE YOU TO DEATH

By Destiny J

I RIDE FOR MY HITTA

I STILL RIDE FOR MY HITTA

By **Misty Holt**

LOVE & CHASIN' PAPER

By **Qay Crockett**

TO DIE IN VAIN

By **ASAD**

BROOKLYN HUSTLAZ

By **Boogsy Morina**

BROOKLYN ON LOCK I & II

By **Sonovia**

GANGSTA CITY

By **Teddy Duke**

A DRUG KING AND HIS DIAMOND

A DOPEMAN'S RICHES

By Nicole Goosby

BOOKS BY LDP'S CEO, CA$H

TRUST IN NO MAN

TRUST IN NO MAN 2

TRUST IN NO MAN 3

BONDED BY BLOOD

SHORTY GOT A THUG

THUGS CRY

THUGS CRY 2

THUGS CRY 3

TRUST NO BITCH

TRUST NO BITCH 2

TRUST NO BITCH 3

TIL MY CASKET DROPS

RESTRAINING ORDER

RESTRAINING ORDER 2

IN LOVE WITH A CONVICT

Coming Soon

BONDED BY BLOOD 2

BOW DOWN TO MY GANGSTA

True Savage 3